Mystery Ham
Hammond, Gerald, 1926-
The fingers of one foot

THE FINGERS OF ONE FOOT

Recent Titles by Gerald Hammond from Severn House

THE FINGERS OF ONE FOOT

Gerald Hammond

This first world edition published 2009
in Great Britain and in the USA by
SEVERN HOUSE PUBLISHERS LTD of
9–15 High Street, Sutton, Surrey, England, SM1 1DF.
Trade paperback edition published
in Great Britain and the USA 2009 by
SEVERN HOUSE PUBLISHERS LTD

British Library Cataloguing in Publication Data

Hammond, Gerald, 1926–
    The Fingers of One Foot.
    1. Authors – Fiction. 2. Women veterinarians – Fiction.
    3. Grandfathers – Death – Fiction. 4. Villages – Scottish
    Borders (England and Scotland) – Fiction. 5. Scottish
    Borders (England and Scotland) – Social conditions – Fiction.
    6. Detective and mystery stories.
    I. Title
    823.9'14-dc22

ISBN-13: 978-0-7278-6801-5   (cased)
ISBN-13: 978-1-84751-162-1   (trade paper)

All Severn House titles are printed on acid-free paper.

Typeset by Palimpsest Book Production Ltd.,
Grangemouth, Stirlingshire, Scotland.
Printed and bound in Great Britain by
MPG Books Ltd., Bodmin, Cornwall.

FOREWORD

It is sometimes said that nursing is now a job and no longer a vocation, but during a recent, serious illness lasting some months I was looked after by a series of nurses, male and female, one and all doing a skilled and unpleasant job with dedication and good humour.

I would therefore like to dedicate this book to the nurses at Western General Hospital (Edinburgh) and Aboyne Cottage Hospital.

ONE

Roland Fox's neat little house was at the edge of a cluster of similarly small houses. The kitchen and several other windows looked over a pastoral scene of crops and pastures to which he expected soon to become reconciled if not precisely enamoured. Spreading through the valley below were the roofs of Newton Lauder and beyond were the hills of the Scottish Borders.

Roland's admiration for the view was uncomprehending. He could see two different species of farm animals – three if you included a pair of retired Clydesdales grazing contentedly in the middle distance – and five different crops. He had no idea what those crops were but he knew that they had to be different because of the different shades of green and brown. There were patches of woodland and strips of trees. He also knew that such scenes were generally supposed to be beautiful and so he expected to enjoy it and he rather thought that when, if ever, he came to understand the ebb and flow of crops and cattle he too might get pleasure from it. Just at the moment, however, he was looking at the view without quite seeing it. It lacked what he was waiting for. He turned away and went down on his knees again beside the form of a large golden retriever. The dog was gasping for breath but still managed a few strokes of the tail. A sharp rat-tat at the front door brought him to his feet.

The figure on the doorstep was that of a young woman, barely more than a girl. She had, it seemed, just reached maturity. Nature had set out to be good to her. Her figure was enticing – so much so that it even looked good in an unflattering grey dress. Her face came even closer to every man's ideal. Her lips were full. Her eyes, which looked blue in some lights and green in others, were clear and bright. Her legs were bare but well worth a whistle.

Her hair, which fell somewhere between blonde and brown, had been brushed and left. But looks are not all. Jane Highsmith was also intelligent but only vaguely aware of it. This awareness took the form of an unfocussed feeling that other people were either stupid or hiding intelligence out of laziness or some form of misplaced courtesy.

This might well have been the person he had been awaiting but in fact they had never met before. Roland's mind went blank for some seconds. The girl was looking at him curiously. 'I'm sorry,' he said. 'I was expecting the vet and not . . .' He broke off again on the point of saying something about lovely young ladies which might or might not have been appreciated. He had been strictly brought up and, being new to the district, was anxious not to put a foot over the line. 'Somebody so young,' he substituted.

'The curse of my life, looking so young,' Jane said lightly. 'Would it help if I said that I'm nearly a hundred years old?'

Roland looked at her sharply and decided that she was pulling his leg. 'It might,' he said, 'if I believed you.'

She made a small movement with the Gladstone bag. 'I assure you that I'm fully qualified.' Her qualifications had been obtained only very recently but there was no need to mention that. She was in fact very young to have progressed so far but high intelligence, a limpet memory and driving ambition had enabled her to qualify in veterinary science. 'I'm Jane Highsmith,' she said. 'The vet,' she added. 'I live just around the corner from here.'

'I thought the partner's name was Grant.'

'That's me, too. I took my great-grandfather's surname when he adopted me, but after his –' she hesitated, '– his death I went back to my original name.' She looked curiously at Roland. 'Are we going to chat on the doorstep? I was told that there was a patient here in need of my services.'

Roland was jerked back to the there and then. 'Oh God! Yes. Please come all the way in. It's Sandy, my retriever. I don't have a car or I'd have brought him in.'

The houses in Birchgrove had been built to serve

newly-weds and first-time buyers. The hallway was just large enough to give access to two doors and the foot of a narrow staircase. Roland was about to make some deprecating, half apologetic remark but Jane was already in the kitchen and down on her knees. 'He's a big chap, isn't he? No wonder you didn't want to carry him! What happened?'

'I took him for a walk. He was out of my sight for no more than a minute and he came bolting back, yelping. He was gasping but not as much as this.'

While she listened, Jane was continuing her quick examination. Sandy looked up with pathetic eyes, pleading for sympathy, comfort and food. He seemed to be breathing with difficulty. 'Can you hold his jaws open for me?' Jane asked. 'Better that you lose a finger than that I do.'

'He wouldn't do anything like that. He's very gentle, aren't you, old son.' It was noticeable that Roland kept his finger out of danger as far as he could but the big dog submitted without demur to his jaws being opened and a torch shone inside. 'Thought so,' Jane said with satisfaction. She burrowed in her bag and then looked up. 'You were south of here? There's a wasp's byke under the gheen tree. Do you have any vinegar?'

'Vinegar?' Even as he echoed the word, Roland was aware that he was not showing up well. The connection between a sick and possibly moribund dog and a kitchen flavouring had caught him off balance.

Jane's voice showed a proper contempt for his denseness. 'Yes, vinegar. Wasp stings are alkaline. Anything acid will neutralize the venom. Make a dilute mixture and help me to get it down him. Quickly, now.'

Persuading a large golden retriever to swallow a liquid with an unpleasant taste can be a messy business. It was some while before the tiled floor was mopped, the two humans had dried themselves as best they could and the big dog was settled, with the aid of a painkiller, in his basket. His breathing was still laboured but much easier.

Jane moved into a hard kitchen chair. 'I'd expect him to make it on his own from here,' she said. 'Let him rest. You can call me if he develops any complications.'

'I don't have your number.'

She pointed to the window. 'Just put your head out of the back door and shout.'

'You're as close as that?'

'Yes. That's my upstairs window prying over our fence. I saw you move in about a fortnight ago. Now I'd better leave you to get on with it. I'm told that you're a writer.'

He made a wry face. 'Fighting to break into a closed shop.'

'An aspiring writer rather than an actual one?'

He was stung by the amusement in her voice. 'I've had one novel published. Not exactly earth-shaking. But you'll have to be going on your rounds.'

'This was my only call.'

'Then don't go.' He decided to ignore the siren call of his word processor. He was not looking for love or even for sex, but she was a girl and an attractive one and any female companionship would save him from the blank screen. 'Would you like a cup of tea? The kettle's still hot.'

'I'd love one.' She had already studied him surreptitiously. He was, she was pleased to note, not cursed with that male handsomeness that usually put her teeth on edge and her back firmly up by denoting conceit, a sexually predatory nature and an assumption of superiority. That at least was her experience. Instead, he had a face that displayed in a not unpleasing way an amenable character. His eyes were serious but they looked ready to smile. His hair, which was in need of cutting, was fair enough that any stubble should have been invisible, but in fact he needed a shave.

'They told me Fox,' she said. 'Would that be Roland Fox?'

He was suddenly shy, even more so than usual. 'In fact, it would.'

'I've just finished reading *The Temptation*.'

There was a pause. He was determined not to ask what she thought of it.

'Silly title,' she said.

'There I agree with you. I had a much better title in mind

but there was a character's name in it and the publishers were adamant that buyers won't go for books with eponymous titles.'

'Well, I think that's damn silly. Dickens and Shakespeare did it all the time.'

'What was worse was that somebody changed the title without consulting me. The first I knew of it was when my copies arrived.'

He got up with a faint cracking of knees, poured tea and put biscuits into a saucer. He looked fit but obviously he had let up on the exercise recently. She realized that writing would be essentially a sedentary job. 'I think that's just damnable,' she said hotly. 'You should change your publisher.'

'I agree. And believe me, I will when I can. But in this age of recession you've got to top the best-seller list before you can do more than toe the line and tug your forelock, or that's the impression I get.'

She accepted her tea in a mug which bore a cartoon of Goofy and to which somebody had added, on a slant, the word or sobriquet 'Podgy' in Magic Marker. 'What are you writing now?'

He almost flinched. 'I started something but it wasn't going anywhere so I put it on the back burner. Now I find that I don't have an idea in my head that doesn't reek of cliché or plagiarism.'

She nibbled a digestive biscuit while she considered. 'The best ideas always come while you're walking. You won't have found your way around yet. If we meet up dog walking, I'll show you the best ways to go,' she said at last. 'Ways that don't include wasps' nests.'

'That would be very kind,' he said stiffly.

As he spoke he realized that his words, which had been sincere, could be taken for the merest courtesy. During their first few minutes together he had thought that he detected a mutual recognition, but on what level? Not sexual, surely. But liking? Respect? He sought for something to add that would restore or even enhance that momentary exchange of almost subliminal contact.

The pause confirmed Jane's interpretation. At first glance she had experienced an intuitive liking but evidently she was alone in this. *He doesn't have to come if he doesn't want to*, she thought. But it would not do to offend one of her very few clients. Her tea was still too hot to swallow quickly and escape. She felt compelled to extend the conversation.

'What brings you here? I mean, why here to Newton Lauder in particular?'

Roland decided that he might as well explain himself. It would save time and misunderstandings if he let this chatterbox spread the truth instead of allowing his new neighbours to invent and disseminate myths about him. 'An elderly aunt of mine died recently.' The explanation sounded very blunt to his own ears so he added, 'In a foot- note to her will she asked that, once she was gone, we do not use any of the customary euphemisms about death. "If the word death was good enough for the Bible," she wrote, "it will do for me." I thought that that was sensible so I stick to it even if it shocks some people.'

'It doesn't shock me,' Jane said. 'Quite the reverse. A vet gets used to the concept but one has to use a zillion euphemisms – people are often more sensitive about the life of a pet than about their own. Your aunt must have been Miss Carnwath. I remember her. She was an old dear but she preferred to be seen as a holy terror.' There was a faraway look in her eyes. 'I think I'll put a similar clause in my will, if I ever get round to writing one and have something worth bequeathing. I'll make it clear that anyone saying that I've *passed on* or *gone to a better place* loses their legacy.'

Roland was delighted with the concept. 'Will you really?'

Jane decided that an escape clause would be called for. 'Unless,' she said, 'he or she can come up with an im- mediate eulogy in the form of a limerick, and rhyming *died* with *fried* will be strictly forbidden for obvious reasons. But if anyone says *popped her clogs* or *kicked the bucket*, that will be quite acceptable.'

It would be gross exaggeration to suggest that, at that

moment, Roland was impaled by Cupid's dart; but he no longer saw Jane as an intrusive female, reminiscent of the young woman who had so recently let him down, but as a not unattractive person whose sense of humour would mesh with his own. Jane saw the laughter ready to break out of him and decided that anyone who laughed at her jokes had to be a fellow spirit.

'Aunt Daisy scared the hell out of me,' he admitted. 'But at least the house was free and clear of death duties. She must have had a heart as big as Ben Nevis. She made a lot of legacies to her favourite charities. I'm her residual legatee, but by the time it's all settled . . .'

Sandy stirred. In a moment Jane was down on her knees but soon rose again, satisfied. 'Go on,' she said.

Roland had already said more than he intended. In babbling about himself he must be giving the impression of an introverted, egocentric weakling but the damage was already done. 'I could have sold the house and used the money to go on paying rent on my rather squalid little flat in Edinburgh.'

It took Jane a second or two to find a form of words that did not suggest either excessive nosiness or doubt as to his employability. 'You're self-employed, then? You've always been a writer?'

Lacking a polite way to invite her to mind her own business, he embarked on his explanation. 'I wasn't tied down by a job, if that's what you're asking. I'd been working on the rewrite desk of *The Scotsman*, but that seemed a waste of a degree in English. I chucked it and spent three years trying to make it on my own. I tried freelance journalism and made about fifty pee a year. I tried writing serials for the magazines. My first attempt at a novel was a love story that even Mills and Boon declined with thanks. Then I wrote *The Temptation*, because crime always sells. In fact, it's difficult to think of a successful novel that doesn't hinge around a crime. But fiction takes a long time to pay off. After the first advance you get your first royalties a year the following June and Public Lending Rights the February after that. I decided that my best option would be to live rent free in comparative peace and quiet while I got on with the next one. One big snag is that you don't meet people and see things going on. You can't dig up ideas worth writing down, out of a blank mind. I should be looking and listening.'

'I suppose that's so,' Jane said. 'Well, at least you have a dog. A dog's always a first class introduction to people.'

'He – or it – doesn't seem to work that way for me.'

'You met me, didn't you?' Jane pointed out cheerfully.

Roland was not too sure how much of a blessing that would prove. 'You wouldn't happen to know anybody in need of a strong back and a literate mind?'

'I'll keep my ears open.'

She was so helpful that he decided to confess a little more. 'I couldn't grudge Sandy his treatment but I may have a little difficulty with your bill. Send it in anyway and I'll settle it as soon as I can. I hate to admit it, but I'm living literally from hand to mouth.'

Jane sighed and told herself that confession would be good for the soul. 'I hope misery does love company,' she said, 'because I'm in much the same state. The present vet retires in the New Year and I have an agreement to buy the practice. Meantime, the arrangement was that he would give me some locum and out-of-hours work, which I was counting on but it hasn't amounted to much more than a row of beans so far. I took out an endowment policy to cover as much as possible of the payment I have to make in January and it leaves me with zilch to live on. So please don't leap to the conclusion that I can wait at the back of the queue when you're settling your debts.' She got to her feet. 'We're a pair, aren't we? Well, I'm going fishing – the evening rise should start soon and it's one way that I keep the wolf from the door. Could you use a trout?'

'Could I!'

'I'll see what I can do. Now come and give me a leg up. There's a Wendy house the other side of the fence.'

He followed her down the garden and stooped to let her scramble onto his back. She vaulted lightly onto the roof of the Wendy house. 'By the way,' he said, 'what's your other name?'

'I'm Jane. Plain Jane.'

He wanted to say that she wasn't plain at all but the words died unuttered. Perhaps when he had known her for ten times as long he would be able to utter a compliment without feeling that he was showing himself up as a seducer.

TWO

Roland could not have afforded to have his milk or a newspaper delivered; in fact, he managed almost entirely without milk and made use of the newspapers in the public library. He had even considered applying for a paper round of his own but a guarded enquiry had discovered that the earnings would not be worth the loss of sleep or writing time. In the morning his visit to his own front door was in the hope that a cheque might have arrived in payment for some previous article or news item. But the doormat remained disappointingly vacant. He went on to open the door to a morning of slanting sunlight with a vague hope that some miracle might have brought a food parcel or that the milkman might have left a delivery on the wrong doorstep.

The age of miracles, it seemed, was not yet past. A plastic ice cream box on the top step, weighted with a heavy stone against the depredation of the neighbourhood's cats, proved to contain two fat, brown trout already beheaded, tailed and gutted. He snatched them up quickly before a cat or some avian predator could snatch them away from him and he shut them firmly in his fridge against the demands of the evening meal. He gave Sandy his breakfast out in the back garden, because the distancing made it easier to ignore the appetizing smell of the chunks of meat and gravy. Sandy, whose throat seemed to be very much improved, ate gingerly but with appreciation. Roland took his own meal of boiled vegetables from the garden on the kitchen table. His aunt or her gardener, luckily, had left the small garden well stocked with vegetables, but he would have to come up with some money before winter. He was sowing seeds to fill the gaps that he was making, but his only advice was contained in the printing on the seed packet which, like most of its kind, began by assuming that the reader was already at least half expert. In his ignorance he was unsure whether any seedlings would reach edibility before next spring.

'You cost more to feed than I do,' he told Sandy, 'so when starvation sets in guess which one of us gets eaten first.' Sandy only thumped his big tail. There was always food. Why should now be different?

Roland had made up his mind to give Jane a suitably fulsome phone call of thanks after walking Sandy, but this proved unnecessary. He always hesitated before making phone calls early in the morning in case the recipient had had a late night and intended to sleep in. He set off to give Sandy his morning walk but they had only reached the first corner when Jane, accompanied by a handsome but ageing Labrador, fell into step with him. This he put down to happy coincidence. Only later did he realize that from her bathroom window she could follow the progress of his morning's preparations and judge her moment for leaving the house. She waved aside his expressions of gratitude. 'Fair exchange,' she said. 'Your aunt left you well provided with vegetables. My step-great-grandmother never ate potatoes. I'll settle for a carrier bag of your potatoes. Throw in a cauli and I'll lift some tatties for both of us.'

'We have a deal,' he said.

She nodded. 'We paupers have to live by barter.'

'I've been finding that out. Unfortunately, words aren't a very valuable commodity until you're famous. Where are we going?'

'I said that I'd show you some better dog walking. Also, I wanted to show you something else.' Roland waited but she left it there.

They had left Birchgrove for open country and woodland. The dogs were put on leads while they crossed over the B-road that was the nearest that the area possessed to a main road and were then allowed to run free. The two dogs decided that they could get along. King Coal, Jane's Labrador, was elderly and knew the area well. Sandy, while making little exploratory forays, was generally content to follow the older dog's leadership. As they walked along a narrow but surfaced farm road, a stream tumbled and chortled on their left and sparkled in the sunlight that found its way through the leaves of the beech trees. On their right a slated roof began to rear up, set back among the trees, but before they reached the house she led him to a seat made from a roughly squared tree trunk.

'That was my home until recently,' she said. 'And King Coal's. We stopped calling him Old King Coal when he began to turn grizzled. After my mother died, my great-grandfather took us in, my sister and myself. We called him GG for short.' She sighed. 'I never realized how much I loved him until suddenly he wasn't there. He was a wonder. I used to think that he knew everything but now, looking back, I can see that he did know an awful lot – he said once that that was the duty of the head of the family – but if he was asked anything too difficult he would put off answering or make an excuse to leave the room while he looked up the answer on the Internet.

'He married my step-great-grandmother about seven years ago though they'd had an affair for some time before that. I'm afraid he was a rogue. I'm not supposed to know about him but people let out bits and pieces of the story. He was widowed not long after his marriage. He lived here even then. Where you and I live, Birchgrove, which is less than a mile from here, had been built to suit first-time buyers but the small houses also suited widows and divorcees and he was a handsome old devil. He wore an eye patch most of the time because he'd lost an eye during World War Two and his false eye was never comfortable for long. It gave him a sort of wild, piratical look that women seemed to drool for.

'When they married, I think they already knew that she had cancer. I think the marriage was to give her comfort. She died two years ago. She still owned the house I'm in now and she left it to me, but it was tenanted and the rent went to her favourite charity. The tenant moved quite recently, leaving me with vacant possession. I was seriously consider-ing moving when GG died and that finally decided me.

There had always been tension between my sister and myself, the way siblings are – you know?'

'Not really,' he said. 'I was an only child.'

'Believe me, you haven't missed much. Is your back getting tired?'

'Yes, a bit.'

'Turn back to back with me, that's much more comfortable.' Roland found that it was also much more friendly. 'I think I might have got on with a brother, but Violet and I only managed to rub along for days at a time before another row would blow up.' Jane fell silent, her voice in danger of breaking. She had had a love of her own, but her older sister, as much out of spite as anything else, or so Jane believed, had brought her more practised lures to bear and the two were married. To add to Jane's dismay, the pair seemed happy. The formalities had not yet been completed but it was believed that the house had been left to Violet with a proviso that a home must be available for Jane, but at the death of GG the situation quickly became impossible. The availability of the other house, smaller but unquestionably her own, had seemed to offer a Heaven-sent resolution but she had reckoned without such burdens as the endowment policy, repayment of her student loan, Council Tax and the upkeep of the communal landscaping and garage court.

When she had control of her voice she said, 'Anyway, I knew that GG was devastated, but he had tremendous inner strength. He soldiered on until he died in an accident only three weeks or so ago.'

Roland had a sudden insight. 'That's why you were wearing a grey dress?'

'Clever of you to notice! It's my way of mourning.' She had abandoned the grey dress for jeans and a light sweater, more or less resembling his except that his were older and much tattier.

Roland had been listening, absorbed. The story as it unfolded might form the skeleton of a novel, perhaps a family saga, or at least become a sub-plot to another story. 'You're talking about Luke Grant the photographer, aren't you?

The lady in the corner shop told me a little about him. I think you said you took his name and only reverted to your birth name when he died.'

'He expected it. In fact he referred to me in his will by my birth name as Jane Highsmith. I think he wanted to continue my father's name – his grandson.'

Roland shifted uneasily. The seat was becoming very hard. 'This is interesting,' he said, 'but why are you telling it to me? I begin to sense an ulterior motive. Or am I wrong?'

'No, you're not wrong,' she said. 'I'm telling it to you because I've read *The Temptation*. You're good, by the way.'

Roland was disproportionately pleased by the casual compliment. 'Thank you, ma'am.'

'Isn't that what men are supposed to say after quick sex? But that's not the point. You observed all the little things that give an insight into people and your reasoning was tight and unarguable. Perhaps you should have been a private eye instead of a novelist.'

Roland had sometimes had the same thought but he was not going to be dragooned into spending valuable writing time – if he could think of anything to write about – chasing somebody else's troubles. He moved uneasily on the hard seat. 'Perhaps,' he said warily.

'Let me tell you how GG died,' Jane said, with an apparent change of subject that did not fool Roland for more than a second. He was just curious enough to say, 'Go on.'

'You said that you were looking for another plot for a novel and the only one you've had published so far was a crime story. You might get the plot for another one out of this. You see, GG's death is generally accepted as accidental. I don't believe it, but I think that you could count the people who think the same way on the fingers of one foot. I want to know the truth behind it and I think you're just the chiel to help me find it and you're looking for ideas. It's what they call a win-win situation.'

He glanced at her. She was watching him so hopefully that he had to smile for the first time since they had met. She decided that he had a beautiful smile, almost angelic, showing very straight teeth. For a second or two he was more than handsome, almost beautiful. 'Go on, then,' he repeated. 'Show me the place and tell me about it. Then I'll give you an answer.'

She glanced at the house and instinctively she lowered her voice although its sound could not have travelled so far nor been heard over the burble of the stream. 'I don't want them to know what we're talking about and a gesture could give it away. Let's walk on.'

They rose and returned to the road. The two dogs abandoned their survey of the rabbit holes and fell in with them. The house, as they approached and passed it, proved to be an old but solid looking building of stone and slate on two floors. The neatly spaced windows suggested that there would be no shortage of bedrooms for the average family. The house was old but very well kept. Both ivy and Virginia creeper climbed the walls but each had been trimmed ruthlessly clear of windows and fascias. Roland, whose experience of gardens had been wholly urban, was surprised to see that the house was bordered by lawn and widely spaced specimen trees rather than neat beds of self-conscious looking flowers.

Beyond the house and further along the B-road, the ground rose slightly and they could see that the trees opened out into a mixture of heath, farmland and, on the higher ground in the distance, heather. The stream had at some time found a cleft through the low hump and was now gushing through a miniature, narrow gorge of its own making. A rough path led down from the road and out of sight from the house. Jane led the way beneath the boughs of an enormous cedar of Lebanon, to where a group of smooth boulders provided more seating of a kind. The path continued, crossing the stream three or four metres above the water by a bridge formed from another tree trunk, big brother to their earlier seat, squared by a skilfully handled chainsaw.

'GG planted this tree, umpty umpty years ago. He brought it back as a seedling from one of his trips to take publicity photographs of new hotels.' Jane sighed. 'They found him some way downstream, but it's assumed that he fell from here.

It's about the only place you could fall in from with enough height to dent your skull, which is what's supposed to have happened. The procurator fiscal got the sheriff to record it as an accidental death.

'They found blood and hair on that rock. This was his favourite walk with the dog. There used to be a rope handrail one side but it wore out and broke about a week before the accident. The dog walkers all said that they were going to replace it, but nobody ever did. Not that it would have made any difference. He had a very good head for heights and he knew the path too well to fall off.'

'Was it daylight or darkness?'

'Bright moonlight,' Jane said. 'I walked with him many times. When we reached here he used to make me walk in front of him and he'd rest one finger on my shoulder so that he could steady me if I wobbled.' Her voice was steady but she finished with a sniff.

'Did he use a stick?'

'Only the last few years, when his arthritis was troubling him.'

Roland could envisage only too easily a very old man with arthritis, walking with a stick by moonlight. The moon hiding behind a sudden cloud, or the tree might have thrown a deep shadow. The stick slipping off the edge of a footway that was nowhere more than half a metre wide. Momentary dizziness. The rock that Jane had indicated stood proud in the middle of the tumbling stream, waiting for a falling man to brain himself. He looked for a form of words that would let her down gently and politely. 'There isn't much to go on,' he said. 'Why don't you believe that it was an accident?'

She met his eye squarely but in silence for a full half-minute. He waited, toying with words to describe the shadows and sunshine on the sparkling water. 'This is the bit that's almost impossible to explain,' she said. 'Belief and disbelief. As intangible as faith. Look at it one way and it's no more than hunch or intuition. Look at it the other way and it's compounded out of ten thousand tiny things – the flick of an eye, the comment somebody doesn't make, a hesitation, a sound or smell too faint to register. In the animal world, these are the kind of clues that sometimes give a vet a hint as to what ails a patient who can't speak.'

'Don't say any more. You've made your point. You may also have told me who you suspect. But let's start with open minds.'

'Try to keep your mind open. You may feel alone. Like I said, I think you could count the people who don't believe that it was an accident on the fingers of one foot. You'll help me, then?'

'I'll start and we'll see how we go.' He stood up. 'I'd like to look at the place.'

She pulled him down by the slack of his jumper. 'We're out of sight from the house here,' she said, 'but you'll be in full view as soon as you move. I'd prefer nobody to know that we're taking an interest just yet.'

'I didn't see any signs of life. Would anybody be at home at this time of a weekday?'

'Definitely yes. She's an architectural photographer capitalizing on what GG taught her. He's a perspective artist and model maker. That's how they met. They both work from home just as GG did; but they'll be away on Tuesday and Wednesday, going over to Dublin to discuss doing the presentation material for a proposed new shopping and leisure centre. It'll be a feather in their caps if it comes off, so she was bragging to me about it.'

Roland's interest had been aroused, not by any mystery surrounding the death of Luke Grant but by the tensions within the family. There might well be at least one novel lurking among the sibling squabbles. The probably laborious and unproductive work of studying the area might well be left for a few days in the hope that the investigation might by then be abandoned but he did not want to break off contact. 'We can come back then,' he said. 'Time spent filling in the background wouldn't be wasted. But not here.' Sitting on a cold boulder, in the shade as well as a cool breeze, was losing its charm.

'Over dinner,' she agreed. 'Come round about seven.'

They were concealed from the house by a clump of bushes but they were in full view from a section of road. A car cruised by. It had darkened windows but Jane must have gained the impression that the driver was looking at them. 'Damn it,' she said. 'I didn't want to be seen taking too much interest in where it happened. Gossip flies around like a virus here.'

'They may not see any significance in a man and a girl walking dogs along here,' he suggested.

'You could be right but I'd be amazed.'

THREE

Jane had intended to devote the middle part of the day to all the chores of living. She also hoped to bring her house to a standard that her mother would have considered fit for a male dinner guest, as opposed to a veterinary client, to see. Her plan was spoiled by the arrival of a pair of local children bringing with them a puppy with an indeterminate terrier ancestry, no known identity and a serious wound in its thigh. After she had dealt, as required by her professional obligations, with the wound, identified the pup as probably belonging to a family that had moved away and anyway would not have been willing or even able to pay for the treatment, and she had managed to find a temporary home for it with the local branch of the Canine Defence League, the day had mostly fled.

The pheasant that she had intended for the meal (a souvenir of the pheasant season now long past) was still solid in the midst of her freezer. However, it had for some time been her thrifty habit when gifted with rabbit or pigeon or having had these fall to her own airgun, to turn the mixed meats into pie-fillers along with finely chopped bacon, kidneys, mushrooms in season, certain wild herbs and perhaps an Oxo cube if required. A touch of curry powder was sometimes added in order to moderate the rabbit flavour. On quitting the family home she had brought with her a dozen of these, in freezer bags and single person portions. Two of these were quick to thaw and heat. A delicious smell soon pervaded the house. There was no time for pastry but fresh or frozen vegetables were easily prepared. Fruit, mostly the previous year's windfalls or plucked in the dark over the fences of neighbours, would have to suffice for a sweet course.

When Roland, promptly at seven, presented himself at her door, he was noticeably tidier than before though little

better dressed. He had shaved, which showed at least a will-
ingness to try. The house was filled with a smell that set
him salivating. Jane was wearing a summer frock in
colourful print, so it was evident that each had made an
effort within their means. Roland had even put a nasty dent
in the remains of his benefit by investing in a half bottle
of a red wine that he knew to be good value. Jane, however,
took this off him and placed it firmly on her hall table. 'I'll
save this for an even more special occasion,' she said. She
seated him at the kitchen table but gave him a glass of
something chilled, pale and delicious.

'My elderflower champagne,' she explained. 'It's what I
do best. My elderberry wine is good but slightly tangy, but
I make a home brew that could knock your head off.'

Glancing round, Roland noticed that the kitchen was well
decorated in delicate colours. What he did not realize until
later was that the room had been transformed from a surgery
back into a small kitchen-dining room by the use of cunning
feminine tricks such as covering tiled surfaces with table-
cloths and putting flowers into glass beakers. Beside the
door hung an enlarged head and shoulders colour portrait
of a man with a patch over one eye. He looked so much
the epitome of the stereotypical swashbuckler that it was
only at second or third glance that he realized that the man
was old. 'Your great-grandfather?'

'Yes.'

Given more time, she would have served a vegetable
soup. She filled two plates with the savoury stew and vegetables. He noticed that she had given him slightly the larger
portions. He ate neatly and politely with his mouth tight
shut but he could not prevent little sounds of pleasure
escaping by way of his nose. She accepted them as the
compliment that they were. She topped up both their glasses.

They both ate with too much enjoyment for speech. When
the first rush of appetite was satisfied at last, he said, 'Now
you could tell me about that day.'

Jane nodded but took a few seconds to empty her mouth.
'The domestic situation was becoming a bit fraught so that
I was thinking of moving out anyway. The house still

belonged to GG but he had been feeling his age. He still
pottered with his cameras but not seriously. Mostly he just
walked the dog, my old King Coal, or rested his bones. He
was living like a guest but paying his way; in fact I rather
think that he was virtually keeping the whole household.
But Violet was doing the housekeeping and she resented it.
We did sometimes have domestic help but it's not easy to
get and keep it out in the sticks and it can be expensive.

'That Sunday, GG was in good form. I think Manfred –'
her voice hesitated at the name '– was sulking about something but GG chatted away more cheerfully than I'd known
him do for some time. It was late – it must have been nearly
ten – when he got up to take King Coal for his usual walk.'
Hearing his name the Labrador thumped his tail twice. Jane
paused for thought while she finished the last of her main
course. That year's apples were not yet ripe, but she had
stewed and frozen some of the previous year's crop and she
served them up with the extravagant (in that she had spent
actual money on it) addition of condensed milk.

'Slow down,' Roland said. 'What was he doing during
the day? That could be important.'

Jane paused with a serving spoon in her hand. 'He spent
some time upstairs. I think I heard the loft ladder being
used but I couldn't be sure. Then he went out for the afternoon. He went on foot but he didn't take King Coal with
him, which usually meant that he was going visiting, either
somewhere that dogs aren't welcome or somewhere too far
away. Usually a Labrador could walk a man off his feet;
but dogs age faster than people and they'd reached the stage
at which GG could walk further than King Coal.'

'But you don't know who he visited?'

'Leave that for the moment,' she said. 'I'll let you in on
my guesses later. I'll move on to the evening.

'If daylight hadn't faded away it was so nearly gone that
it was swamped by the moonlight. He knew that I was
physically tired – I'd been on my feet all day, inoculating
a herd of cattle – so he said not to come with him as I
occasionally did, but I made sure that he had his stick and
the rechargeable lantern. He asked me to wait up for him

because he had something to say – I never did hear what. And that was the last I saw of him. After an hour, Manfred went to look for him, carrying the only spare torch, but he came back and said that there was no sign of him, but that King Coal had come back to the front door in a thoroughly upset state.

'The moon had gone in by then so it was almost as dark as it ever gets in summer this far north. The torch had run out of battery so there was nothing much to be done until dawn. I lay down on my bed but I didn't sleep.'

'One moment,' Roland said. Jane, who had been carried along by her story, blinked at him. 'One moment,' he said again. 'What did the others do during that interval?' Jane looked at him in puzzlement. 'You must be wondering if, to put it at its mildest, your sister and her husband didn't have some responsibility.'

Jane got up and poured coffee. 'Yes,' she said vaguely.

Obviously there was more to come. Roland sipped his coffee. 'Real Java,' he said appreciatively. 'This is something I've missed. I've been making do with wishy-washy tea.'

'If you've been a student,' Jane said, 'I'm surprised that you haven't learned all the tricks.' The change of subject, however fleeting, came as a relief. 'I'll tell you this one for nothing on the sole condition that you leave the supermarket in the Square alone, because it's mine. I go through the shelves now and again, looking for items that are just about to go past the sell-by date. One or two other people do the same, but they're looking for treats for dogs or horses. In some places the supermarkets put outdated goods on sale at half price, but hereabouts they're too scared of the authorities. Consumer Protection are absolute tigers. So if you find something that's about to go out of date you can usually talk them into letting you have it for half price or less. That's how I came by some jars of this coffee. I'll give you one, all to yourself.'

'Wow!' said Roland. 'You've brought shoestring living to a fine art.'

'Stick around. You ain't seen nothin' yet. Coming back

to your question, the answer is that I don't know. I could
hear their voices for a while, coming from the sitting room.
I think that they may have dozed in the chairs.

'When I saw daylight making a return I got up and
washed. I think that Vi had given up and gone to bed by
then. I phoned the police to let them know that an elderly
gentleman was missing and then I borrowed one of GG's
walking sticks and went out to look for myself. I took King
Coal with me. One of the local bobbies turned up almost
immediately and we walked together, discussing what on
earth could have happened to GG. King Coal stopped before
we got to the bridge and wouldn't come any closer – it was
several days before he could be walked over the bridge.
Manfred must have got up and followed me out. We met
him near the bridge and we searched around together, paying
particular attention to the water. We found the lantern just
below the bridge. It was still switched on but it wasn't
working. At that time we must have been quite close to
GG, but we learned later that he'd drifted into the bank
where a lot of grass and weeds overhung the water. It was
only later when a proper search—'

She was interrupted by a musical ring on the doorbell.
Again the interruption came as a relief, because her voice
was on the point of being choked by tears. 'I seem to be
in demand.' Excusing herself she rose and trotted to the
front door. Roland could hear the voice of the woman visitor.
'Can you help me please, Jane? Jack's got something in
his eye.'

'Yes, of course. Come through to the kitchen.'

Jane reappeared moments later accompanied by an older,
very well groomed woman and a springer spaniel.
Somewhere along the way, Jane had gathered up her medical
bag. She produced a torch and went down on her knees.
The springer, obviously distressed, was fighting against the
urges to blink and rub its eye. Speaking soothingly, Jane
drew back its upper eyelid. 'A gorse prickle,' she said.
'Nasty! Hold her head as still as you can.' Without releasing
the eyelid, she plucked a pair of tweezers from her bag and
deftly removed a tiny thorn from the eye, replacing it with

some ointment from a nearly empty tube. 'That should do for now,' she said. 'I wouldn't expect any more trouble but you'd better let Mr Hicks look at it in the morning.'

'Couldn't you—?'

'Until I take over, I'm supposed to limit myself to emergencies and occasions when he isn't available. That was the agreement.'

'Well, it seems a pity. He can be hard to get hold of.'

'It's not just that I'm cheaper?'

The visitor laughed. 'I can take a hint,' she said, picking up her handbag. 'How much do I owe you?'

'Could we borrow Ronnie Fiddler for a day or two?'

'Which day or two?'

'Tuesday and possibly Wednesday.'

'That will be all right. So you're looking into your great-grandfather's accident, are you?'

Roland thought that he saw Jane stiffen. 'Why should you think that?'

The older woman smiled. 'Why else would you want to borrow Ronnie? He acts as my butler and general man-servant now, but he spent much of his life as my grandfather's ghillie and stalker and he still takes parties up into the hills. Unless you're preparing to give a dinner party I can only suppose that you want him for his tracking skills. He's still good if you don't hurry him. Borrow him by all means. I was never quite convinced that your great-granddad fell by accident, no matter what that damn fool sheriff said. There's no charge for his services but I insist to paying for yours.' She took a note from her bag and pressed it into Jane's hand.

Jane made a small gesture of surrender, tucking the note under a jar on a shelf. 'And here I was, telling Roland that people who, like me, disagreed with the fiscal's view were as rare as the fingers on one foot. This is my neighbour Roland Fox,' she said. 'Roland, this is Mrs Ilwand. Roland's had a crime novel published, so I'm persuading him to help me . . .'

'To investigate?'

'Well, yes.'

'Let me know if I can help in any other way.' Mrs Ilwand glanced out of the window. She seemed to be looking into the past or, Roland thought, into the might-have-been. Her face softened. 'I had a soft spot for your great-grandfather. He was very good to me. I treasure the shots that he took of my favourite dogs. You know, you mightn't have been aware of it, but he had the most overpowering sex appeal. Sometimes I thought that you could actually smell the testosterone. If he'd made the least move in my direction, when I was a student . . . You're not hearing this,' she added to Roland. 'GG must have been nearly fifty years older than I was but he made my knees go wobbly. All the girls in the town lusted after him but he only seemed to go for ladies nearer to his own age, which made him close to unique.'

While Jane saw the other woman with her spaniel to the door, Roland brooded. Mrs Ilwand's parting words had set him thinking. Hell might have no fury like a woman scorned, but surely a man of great age was out of that particular danger? Life was so unfair. Why should one man be gifted with so much sex attraction over so many years? And where had it gone to, now that he'd finished with it? He glanced up at the photographic self-portrait of Luke Grant that hung beside the door and wondered whether the eye patch was part of the secret, suggesting as it did a background of dangerous adventure. Perhaps if he took to wearing an eye patch . . . He would cheerfully sacrifice an eye in exchange for the power to fascinate women. A writer could manage perfectly well with one eye or none at all. Milton had been blind . . .

In his bed that night he resumed his ruminations on the subject. In his fantasy, fuelled as it was by elderflower champagne, he imagined having such a power over women. A wink, a lopsided smile or a blown kiss and she would be his to do with as he would. His imaginary partner, though lacking a positive identity, bore a strong resemblance to Jane.

FOUR

By the time that they parted to go to their separate beds and their highly individual dreams, they had added a great deal of fact and speculation on the only blank paper to come to hand – the reverse sides of Roland's university notes on The Influence of Lloyd Osborne on his Stepfather.

Roland had assumed that their discussion would be resumed during a morning dog walk, but there was no sign of Jane or of King Coal as he walked Sandy along to the log bridge and back. The day was calm and warm, filled with the scents of summer. It was possible that Sandy, who had lived his life in Edinburgh, had never seen a rabbit but, driven by instinct, he was hunting them now.

Roland was most of the way home and Birchgrove was well in sight before Jane came in view, emerging from the trees in the direction of the hospital. She gave him a friendly wave and waited until he came up with her. King Coal was lagging slightly so Roland concluded that she had walked further than usual. The two dogs greeted each other.

'I went to intercept a friend of mine,' Jane said. 'Simon Parbitter. Do you know him?'

'Not to say know.' Suppressing a little pang of envy, Roland decided to be honest. 'I've read a lot of his stuff. He's good.'

'Isn't he, just! He lives a couple of miles up the hill. Keeps Labradors, so there can't be much wrong with him.' Roland looked at her but she seemed perfectly serious. 'Anyway, I didn't say anything to you because I didn't want to raise false hopes, but you do seem to be chronically short of funds. So it occurred to me that you might be able to use some paid work. You don't mind?'

'Mind what?'

'Me, jumping to conclusions.'

'Not in the least. You're absolutely right. Conclusions are for jumping to. Anyway, you didn't jump to any conclusions; I broke the sad news myself. I could certainly use some paid work provided only that it doesn't call for the use of muscles or skills I've never developed.'

'This would be right up your street.'

Without any particular intention they had drifted to a halt outside Jane's house. 'Come in for coffee,' she said. 'Dogs are always welcome. Do you mind my asking, why are you so broke? On the other hand, why did you give up your job if you're almost penniless? It does seem to show a certain lack of forethought.'

It took him the three paces along her short hall to decide again on frankness. In her bright kitchen he slumped into a hard chair. 'It looks that way,' he said. 'But there's something you don't know – something I didn't know until after I'd chucked my job and they'd hired a successor. I had a girlfriend.'

'You don't have to go on,' Jane said. 'All is explained.'

'No it is not,' he said. He tried not to sound irritable but without, he thought, success. 'Her existence was only the tip of the iceberg. Her deeds were more drastic. She was quite beautiful, slim and with a face of angelic innocence. Her smile made you want to wrap her in cotton wool to protect her from this naughty world.' For a few moments Roland allowed himself to drift back on the tide of memories. Then he pulled back. 'I thought that I was the luckiest man alive and I thought that she was of the same mind. I had no warning at all until I came home from work one day to find that she'd gone. All her clothes had been taken and most of mine. I spotted some of mine later in a second-hand shop. All the furniture had gone, the kitchen equipment, the television, the video, the car, everything that we had on hire purchase, leaving me stuck with the payments.'

Jane checked an involuntary movement of her hand towards him. 'That is not good,' she said.

'There's worse. She'd drawn cash on our joint credit cards up to the limit and cleared out our accounts. The mortgage on our flat was almost paid off but she'd remortgaged it up to the hilt. According to the police, I'm not the first man that she's cleaned out but they still can't find her. I knew her as Janice Carpenter but the police had nearly a dozen other names for her though they wouldn't tell me any of them.'

'I'm sorry,' Jane whispered. 'So sorry. I apologize on behalf of the entire female sex. I shouldn't have opened the wound.' She blew her nose noisily. She really must conquer this humiliating tendency to shed real tears of sympathy. There was a prescription that she used for watery eyes in dogs; perhaps she should give it a try. 'I just hope that my news helped a little bit.'

'What news? You haven't told me yet.'

'I haven't? It seems trifling after what you've been put through. But you know Simon Parbitter?'

'You asked me that before. You said that he lives near here.'

'So I did. Your tale of woe drove everything else out of my head. I went to see Simon because you can never reach him on the phone – his wife's a sweetie but as far as she's concerned he must never be interrupted while he's writing, so it's quicker to walk up the hill and knock on the door or yoo-hoo through the letterbox until he comes to the door.'

'Forgive my mentioning it, but you still haven't told me what you're talking about.'

Jane knuckled her forehead. 'Proofreading or copy-editing, that's what I'm talking about. Simon's prolific when the ideas are flowing and he resents wasting time and mental energy on books that he's already written and moved on from. He'd love to have another writer do his copy-editing and proofreading for him – somebody who knows the language and can be trusted to spot omissions or contra-dictions, discuss what he thinks are mistakes and not to correct the grammar within quotes or commit any of the other deadly sins. He's prepared to pay quite well by my standards but you may not agree, so he wants to meet you. But he was quite clear about one thing. No money up front. Do the work first and then get paid.'

'I'd expect that,' Roland said. 'But this is great! I can be earning while I sit at my desk and let my subconscious hunt around for ideas. The only snag could be that style can be very infectious, but he writes clear and perfect English without a very strong style. His rhythm's much the same as mine.'

'I don't know whether it would start immediately. I think he's almost ready to be helped with copy-editing.'

'Now is when I'm hungry,' Roland said. 'But I dare say that I can survive, with your guidance.'

Obviously he needed to be taken firmly in hand. 'Of course you can –' She paused on the point of emphasizing her words with a mild expletive. Either he had due regard for her gender or he had been delicately reared. Either way, she had never heard him swear and it seemed early to dispel his illusions. '– survive,' she said. 'Do you fish?'

'No.'

'Shoot?'

'No.'

'Then either you come out with me and learn or your survival will be of the vegetarian kind. Those are two hobbies that can be expensive or rewarding, depending on how you go about them. And if you run short of garden produce you may have to start selling bits of yourself to medical science or for transplanting. I'm joking,' she added as he changed colour. 'We won't let it come to that. I'll tell you what. Tomorrow I have to go up to the moors to test three cows for TB. Mr Hicks can't be bothered to go so far for so little work. The rest of the day's our own. That farm's overrun with rabbits. We could take my air rifle and get a few for our respective freezers.'

He wrinkled his nose. 'I could get hungry enough to eat the leg of a table but I don't think I could eat rabbit. I had a neighbour once who used to boil rabbits to feed his ferrets and I never got used to the smell.'

'He must have let them get a bit rank. What do you think we ate last night?'

'That was rabbit? I thought it was curried chicken.'

'That was rabbit, plus some wood-pigeon meat, onion and a pinch of curry powder. Go ahead and starve if that's what you want but Sandy won't be so fussy and he depends on you. Tell me, since we seem to be exchanging confidences, how did you come to be called Roland?'

'Don't you like it?'

'I love it. Knights in armour, gallant deeds and maidens in distress. It just seems rather old-fashioned.'

He shrugged. 'My mother was a romantic. *Child Rowland to the dark tower came. King Lear.* I've got used to it now.'

'You wouldn't prefer to use your middle name – if you have one?'

He shuddered. 'That's worse.'

'Tell me anyway.'

'I keep that as my dark and dirty secret.'

'I'll find out in the end. I always do.'

Their day out was both enjoyable and profitable. Jane fetched an elderly Terios. A vet, she explained, might manage without any other luxuries but a car was an absolute essential. The crumbs that fell from the boss's table often did so because trips into the countryside might be less profitable than consultations in his surgery. She kept its use to a minimum but it was kept fuelled at half the current rate in payment for regular maintenance inspections of the trio of service station guard dogs that nobody else felt brave enough to approach.

Driving very gently to conserve precious fuel, Jane took them deep into the Lammermuir hills. Roland proved competent with the air rifle, so Jane let him shoot from the concealment of a tumbledown byre while she worked. The dogs were allowed to retrieve the slain, a task at which Sandy proved competent and which King Coal tackled carefully but with a zest suggesting that good times had come again. A breeze was blowing gently across close-cropped grass and heather. While the rabbits cooled in the shade the humans were treated to tea and a sandwich by the farmer's wife. Jane had brought with her a supply of freezer bags, a sharp knife and a cool box with a bag of ice. Roland at first jibbed at the task of skinning, gutting and jointing his bag, but he soon overcame any nausea at the smell and the unpleasantness of the associations. A skinned rabbit might bear a distressing resemblance to a tiny human but he concentrated on remembering the previous night's feast. Nobody, so far as his reading had revealed, had ever seen an undernourished cannibal.

As they returned towards home, comfortably aware of a valuable stock of meat to share between their freezers, Roland said that he had been thinking. 'About ways to make an elderly man fall off a log in the dark. I see now where the expression about *falling off a log* comes from. The notes we made don't go half far enough.'

'Go ahead,' Jane said. 'Amplify.'

'My lecturers would have doted on you. Never a word wasted. Most unusual for a woman.' Jane let the slur go past, quite accepting that while a man would hurry to the guts of his story the average woman would wish to convey every corroborative detail as she went along. Roland dug into his pockets for some paper and a ballpoint pen. 'Drive gently and warn me of any bumps to come. There's no harm repeating what we thought of last night. Heading One, Accident. Did he lose his balance and fall?'

Jane reminded herself that this was an academic enquiry and nothing to do with her much loved ancestor. 'His doctor gave evidence at the Fatal Accident Inquiry. She said that his blood pressure was that of a man less than half his age. She could think of no reason for a dizzy spell.'

'I take it . . . Old people sometimes take to drugs to control pain.'

The car wavered in its course. 'I would have known,' Jane said. 'Anyway he didn't have pain. He was still as fleet as a fifty-year-old. Well, almost. He was slowing down, there's no denying it, but he was steady on his feet.'

'All right. But it's still possible for somebody to trip.'

'I thought of that.' They were still on a single-track road with passing places. A rusty van was struggling up the hill towards them. Jane stopped in one of the passing places to let it grind past in a gust of burning oil. 'The walking surface is smooth.'

'Shoelace?'

'As he got stiffer in his old age he found shoelaces a drag. He took to elastic-sided boots with Velcro fastening.' Her car was too old for air conditioning and it was heating up under the sun. She lowered the windows and pulled out onto the road.

Roland turned over his paper to find a clean side. 'An accident is still possible if we just haven't thought of the right one yet. But we'll move on. Heading Two, Direct Attack. In poor moonlight, anyone dressed entirely in grey and with a grey hood might approach fairly close without being seen.'

'Not in black?'

'Black shows up more than grey in a feeble light. Or he could drop out of the tree.'

'Onto a narrow log bridge?' Jane said. A wood pigeon was idling in the road. She slowed to let it get clear. 'Very uncertain. Give that one a question mark. I could more easily imagine somebody lurking under the bridge and reaching up to grab his ankle or leaning down from the tree and swinging a club.'

'Well done! Two-two. That's the kind of thinking we need. We'll have to look again at the contours to see whether there's anywhere that a man could stand with a long pole.'

'I don't think that there is, but we'll look anyway. Let's move to the area that I think most hopeful. Heading Three. Projectiles. I suppose that somebody standing up on the opposite bank could have thrown a large stone with a good chance of connecting even in the poor light, but I'm thinking more along the lines of a pebble fired from a catapult or some sort of crossbow. If he hit his head when he fell among the rocks, who could find another small dent?'

They had come down off the moors and almost rejoined the main road. The roofs of Newton Lauder, the woods and lush farmland were below and ahead of them. Jane signalled and swerved into the last of the passing places. She set the handbrake, stopped the engine and put her head down on the wheel. Roland waited patiently. He was not surprised. Beyond the town he could see over rolling countryside – almost, he thought, to the sea.

'I'm sorry,' she said at last in a tremulous whisper. 'I know I asked you to . . . But it suddenly rolled over me that we're talking about GG. My great-grandfather. The person I loved most in the whole world. If I'm right, somebody took his life away from him. Perhaps he couldn't have had much life left to look forward to, but he enjoyed it and I was happier for having him around.'

'I know,' he said. He wondered how to offer comfort, but when he put his arm across her shoulders she shook him off angrily. He drew patterns on his paper while she gave way to grief. She had no way to tell him, but his restraint was an enormous mark in his favour. 'Perhaps,' he said at last, 'your great-grandfather had a painful and lingering death ahead of him and his killer, without realizing it, gave him a quick and merciful end instead.'

'Perhaps,' Jane whispered. She sounded unconvinced. 'But perhaps he'd have liked to see me being married. He'd have wanted to walk me down the aisle . . . if that time ever comes. Did you say something?'

Roland had been on the point of assuring her that she would not be allowed to die a spinster, but he told her that he had not spoken.

FIVE

Ronnie Fiddler turned out to be as remote as could be imagined from Roland's mental picture of the butler to one of the local landowners. He was a large, elderly man in stiff and hairy tweeds. The man was just as stiff and hairy as his tweeds and, even allowing for his beginnings as a stalker and ghillie, surprisingly rough-hewn in appearance. Despite the heat of the day he wore a waterproof shooting jacket with many pockets. He seemed unfamiliar with the horn-rimmed spectacles perched on his nose. His speech was not the half-Northumbrian speech of the Borders locally (where a coat is a *coh-wut*) but was heavily laden with the much less comprehensible Doric of the north-east. This, however, the reader may well be spared, taking both accent and dialect on trust. He presented himself at Jane's house early on the Tuesday morning. The two were old friends, Ronnie having taught Jane to cast a very pretty fly-line even before her figure had blossomed and Jane having more recently recovered for Ronnie the artificial flower, swallowed by his lurcher, that Ronnie had worn to a number of past weddings and that he still hoped to wear to several more including, as he said, Jane's.

When Roland turned up, the two were seated in Jane's kitchen with mugs before them and enjoying a blether about old times. Rural tradition demanded that, by the time that introductions had been made, Ronnie had been apprised of much of Roland's earlier history and his connections in the Newton Lauder area. Once Roland's identity had been established satisfactorily, Ronnie said (as translated from his broad Scots), 'And what am I to do for you? The mistress only said to give you all the help I could.'

'I'm still fretting over my great-grandfather's death,' Jane said. 'I'm just not convinced that it was an accident, no matter what the sheriff recorded.'

Ronnie nodded wisely. It seemed that he was one of the fingers on Jane's mythical foot. 'No more am I. See, I knew your great-granddad. Not long back, when he was taking the photos for that book about country sports, he asked could he come with me when I took a visitor stalking. He was an old man by then and I thought I'd maybe have to give him a piggyback, but not a bit of it. We took him as high as we could in the Argocat and then we walked. He was a bit slow, mind, and we had to give him time, but he managed. Then, the way the wind was and the way the beasts were settled, we had to work our way round the face of a crag. I didn't fancy it much. I could see the visitor was scared but he wasn't going to show it in front of us. Your great-granddad, though, he set off as sure-footed as a mountain goat and soon he was telling me where to set my feet. Unless there was a sad change to his health in the last year or two—?'

'Nothing like that,' Jane said. 'He was ageing, of course, but he crossed that bridge several times a day and I never saw him waver.'

'There you are, then. With his head for heights and his sense of balance, he could have walked a tightrope. Unless a bird flew in his face, of course.'

Jane and Roland exchanged a look. Roland opened his binder and added that suggestion.

'Or a bat,' said Jane.

Ronnie shook his head. 'Bats have their own radar. I never knew one to touch a person and never mind what they say about them tangling in a lady's hair. Owls have grand night vision – I wish I had as good. But when other birds, like swallows, are still taking flying insects, sometimes they'll collide with a person in the half light or moonlight. That could knock you off balance. Dashed unlikely, though.'

'That's what I thought,' Jane said. 'Let's go and look at the place. We're hoping that you haven't lost your tracking skills since your days as a stalker.'

Ronnie drew himself up and looked at her as he might have looked at an impertinent four-year-old. 'My skills are as good as ever they were,' he said. 'Whether the signs are still there to be seen, that's another matter. You should ha' called me in three weeks back.'

'Of course,' said Jane. 'Let's go and see.'

Ronnie shook his head. 'First, tell me what you think I'm looking for.'

The dogs had already had their morning walk. They were confined together on Jane's lawn and warned of terrible reprisals if they should manage to stray.

At Jane's gate stood an old and rusty Land Rover. Jane sniffed suspiciously at an open window but it had been some years since the vehicle had carried fish or other quarry. The smell might have blown away but the rusty patches had not healed up. Jane declined the offered lift on the grounds that she preferred not to draw attention to their enquiries. She collected her camera in the faint hope that they would find something worth recording and they set off on the ten-minute walk.

It was clear that Jane's sister and her brother-in-law were, as she had predicted, away from home. She rapped on the door and then used her key but the house was empty.

Where the path across the bridge diverged from the road, Ronnie called a halt and walked on alone. Jane made a small sound of annoyance as a figure arrived over the hump. The figure belonged to a slim man in middle age with thinning silver hair. Jane and Roland looked down into the stream and conversed, intelligently on Jane's part, about the possibility of brown trout. The man glanced at them through horn-rimmed glasses and nodded as he strode by, swinging a light walking stick. He knocked on the door of Whinmount and then, receiving no answer, put an envelope through the letter slot and retraced his steps, nodding again as he passed by and disappeared over the hump.

'Damn!' said Jane.

'Who was it?'

'Don't know for sure. If it's who I think it is, he's a terrible gossip. I'd prefer that nobody saw us messing around here. I don't want to set people talking until we're good and ready.' Roland decided that she was sensible. He could well imagine the complications once all and sundry knew that they were retracing the steps of the police. There would be critical comments, helpful suggestions and fragments of information of questionable accuracy.

When he was satisfied that there was nothing to be learned from the short and twisty path between the road and the bridge, Ronnie beckoned them forward and nodded them to the seat where they had lingered once before. 'You two bide here a few minutes,' he said. 'I'll be back.'

He walked forward, first studying the ground and then pausing to look intently up into the branches of the cedar tree. He gave the surface of the bridge more than a passing glance and walked on more slowly, studying the ground and its traces but also looking back towards the bridge. Nearly half an hour had passed before he returned to the others. He made a wordless sound expressing disbelief. 'Tell me again what you think I'm looking for.'

Roland produced a printout of his list.

Ronnie folded it up and handed it back. 'There's been nobody climbed the far slope for a year or more,' he said, 'and that's the one place a catapult could have been fired from. There's a hollow on top of that wee knoll and folk have been coming and going by the far side, but it's too far off for a catapult. A stone-throwing over that distance I just cannot believe. I could maybe imagine a round pebble wrapped in paper or cotton and fired out of a shotgun.'

'We'd have heard a shot,' Jane said.

'Were you along with them when they searched the water downstream?'

'Most of the way,' said Jane.

Ronnie squatted down on his heels in the position that comes easily to one who has spent his life outdoors but soon becomes insufferable to others. 'Tell me what they found.'

Jane uttered a wordless sound expressing contempt. 'They found heaps of evidence that people are dirty bastards but a lot of it would have come down from further upstream. Several carrier bags. I remember one or two children's toys and things like old gloves and a scarf. There were also a few thingies.' Jane stopped and bit her lip.

'I think she means condoms,' said Roland.

Ronnie nodded. 'Aye. There would be. Nothing bigger?'

'There was an empty oil drum – a small one, four or five gallons – and a supermarket trolley. And there was the top part of an old pram – I suppose they'd kept the bottom part to make a cart – what they call a hurley. I'm sorry, but that's all I can remember.'

'You've done fine. Seems to me,' Ronnie said, pointing above his head, 'that the tree's the place.'

Roland looked doubtfully at Ronnie, who seemed to be ageing visibly, and asked, 'Shall I climb up and look?'

Ronnie had already stooped to his laces. He kicked off his boots, gave Roland one disparaging look, pressed his spectacles more firmly onto his nose and then jumped. Catching the overhead branch he chinned himself and then in one fluid movement he was sitting on the branch. Roland was in no doubt of having committed a faux pas.

Jane decided on a gesture to save Roland's face. 'Your arthritis is better then?' she asked.

'Not a damn bit. But I'm my old self so long as I don't bend or twist to either side. I can see marks in the lichen.' He climbed more carefully, higher, out over the water. 'Somebody climbed in shoes. And there's a thin cut into the bark. What happened to that oil drum? Did the police take it away?'

'Damned if I know,' Jane said. 'They didn't seem to see any significance in it and it isn't their job to tidy the place. The last I saw of it, it was left on the bank.'

'More fools them,' Ronnie said. 'You know where it is. Go and fetch it, there's a good quinie, but first hand us up your wee camera.'

Roland rather felt that he would not trust the other man with anything as delicate even as a crowbar, especially while balanced precariously in a tree over water, but Ronnie accepted the little digital camera in his big paws and seemed quite familiar with its operation. Roland was left to sit on his uncomfortable boulder in puzzlement and frustration while Ronnie moved from branch to branch, taking photographs with what seemed to be a steady hand. The camera he could recognize as being of very high quality. Roland could see no pattern or logic in the sequence of photographs but the scenery, which had seemed at first to his urban eyes to be no more than a chocolate-box assembly of features, began to make sense to him as an outcome of natural events and so to reveal an underlying beauty.

Jane appeared on the far bank, lugging a blue-painted, rectangular drum. At the same time a voice called from the road. 'What on earth are you doing up there? Come down at once before you fall and hurt yourself, man.'

For lack of any constructive action available to them, Jane and Roland, who could neither see or be seen, remained still and silent. Jane at least recognized the voice and its carefully cultivated accent and could picture the newcomer, who was a plump lady in her mid-forties. She was dressed in art silk to suit the warm weather but with more frills and flounces than suited her age or the time of day. She was accompanied by an apricot standard poodle on a pink lead. The poodle was neatly clipped but not in the full French style.

The lady's supercilious manner put Ronnie's back very firmly up. It was immediately clear that he resented being addressed as *man,* aspersions being thrown on his agility and being given orders by one who was not entitled to any authority over him. In his indignation his dialect slipped so far back to the Doric of his youth that Roland could only understand bits of it and guess at the rest, but light was thrown on the lady's origins by the fact that she seemed to understand and resent every word. Roland soon inferred from the lady's shrill and indignant reply, which included the threat of a complaint to Mrs Ilwand, that she had been invited to go away and mind her own business.

Jane snorted. 'It's Mrs Cadwallader,' she murmured, 'and this has gone far enough. Perishing bad luck!' She pushed herself to her feet and walked towards the road. 'Mrs Ilwand kindly lent us his services for a rather confidential matter,' she announced. 'I'll be very grateful if you'll leave us to get on with it and say nothing to anybody.'

If Jane hoped to choke the other off and obtain her silence, the hope was immediately seen to be futile. 'Oh, it's you, Jane dear. What on earth are you up to? It's not like you to be so secretive.' This was followed by more in the same vein; indeed it seemed that Mrs Cadwallader was prepared to continue indefinitely without any change to the basic message but expressing it in an infinite number of variations.

Jane decided that the damage was already done. The news of the activity around the bridge would soon be common knowledge and any neighbour with a modicum of intelligence would be able to guess the purpose. With some difficulty she broke in on the monologue. 'If you'd like to come away from the road and join us,' she said, 'I'll explain – while Ronnie gets on with the job,' she added with emphasis.

The invitation was accepted and Mrs Cadwallader began to pick her way down the uneven path. Roland noticed that her shoes were a compromise between smart and sensible. She chose the smoothest of the boulders and dusted it off with a handkerchief before lowering her well cushioned bottom onto it. She then had attention to spare for her introduction to Roland. It was clear that his name meant nothing to her and his only significance was a romantic one. 'Is this the new man in your life, dear?' she asked coyly.

Jane managed not to grit her teeth while sparing Roland an apologetic glance. 'Mr Fox is a neighbour who kindly agreed to help me. I'm trying to satisfy myself that there was nothing untoward about my great-grandfather's death.'

'But of course there was nothing *untoward* as you put it.' Mrs Cadwallader was evidently incensed on behalf of everybody who might have been involved. 'The sheriff already decided so. And even if your great-granddad decided to end his own life, which is most unlikely because he was an essentially happy man, it would be a most unlikely way to do it. And it's impossible to imagine anybody wanting to give him a push. He was such a gentleman,' Mrs Cadwallader said with a faint blush, 'always friendly, always polite, always helpful. Always so *nice,*' she added as if that said it all. 'But, that said, he was so steady on his feet that you can't imagine him falling off. I've seen him stand on a chair to change a light bulb and he never wobbled even once.'

Mrs Cadwallader had touched on every possible outcome without discounting any of them so that Jane felt quite entitled to probe further. 'You sometimes walk Fifi this way of an evening.'

'Sometimes,' the older woman agreed. 'More often I go the other way, between the farms where there's never any traffic and I know more of the people I'm likely to meet.'

'And on the night my great-grandfather died? You must remember, because the whole area was buzzing with the news next day.'

'Yes, of course I remember. I'm not senile yet, you know. I did come this way that evening but much earlier because I had a gentleman coming to dinner. I must have come past here at about six going out and perhaps six-thirty going home. And I would certainly have noticed if somebody had been lurking in the branches of the tree, waiting to give your great-grandfather a clonk with some sort of a club. Anyway, he wouldn't know what time Mr Grant would have come by here and if he'd stayed up there for hours somebody would have been bound to see him, just as I did even if he wasn't as bulky as Mr Fiddler up there, so you can put that out of your mind.' With the air of one who had set the rest of the world to rights and also gained the last word, Mrs Cadwallader got to her feet, twitched the poodle's lead and prepared to depart.

Jane resented the other's patronizing tone but she was handicapped by not knowing what theory Ronnie was about to expound; and even if she had known she would not have been prepared to divulge it. She returned instead to an earlier observation by the other woman. 'Whinmount has wall-mounted lights downstairs,' she said, 'except in the kitchen which has a double fluorescent strip. The only ceiling fixtures are upstairs, in the bedrooms. When were you in my great-grandfather's bedroom?'

The blow found a mark. Mrs Cadwallader changed colour and gobbled for a few seconds. 'It was a long time ago,' she said at last. 'He wanted my advice about colour schemes. Anyway,' she added, much too late, 'it was in somebody else's house altogether.' As she climbed the path to the road the gyration of her buttocks managed to express indignation, apology and at the same time a degree of self-satisfaction.

Jane called after her, 'Can you tell me who else takes an evening walk this way?' She got no answer. 'I know them anyway,' she told Roland. 'There are only one or two.'

The rhythm of a walker's footsteps sounded on the road and there was the patter of a dog's paws and a whistle. 'That's Mr Hepplestone from next door but one to you,' Jane murmured. 'You can hear his bulldog wheezing. But he never walks after dark.'

SIX

Ronnie had not allowed Jane's discussion with Mrs
Cadwallader to interrupt his exploration of the
branches. He had been easing himself from branch
to branch, studying the signs and occasionally bracing
himself against one limb in order to photograph another.
His climbing among the branches was apparently made
without effort although Roland soon came to see that each
move was made after careful choice of those movements
that would not hurt his joints. Once he was sure that the
attention of his companions had been returned to him,
Ronnie said, 'Is the oil drum empty?'

'It is now,' Jane said. 'It only had water in it but it was
heavy to carry and the handle was sharp.'

'M'hm. Fill it half-full of water and pass it up to me.'

Roland was pleased to find a task, other than note-taking,
that was within his competence. Without getting his feet
more than slightly wet, he managed to lower the drum into
the water and to recover it slightly more than half full.
Lacking any cap, it proved a difficult load to convey into
the branches without spilling more over himself. Ronnie
managed to carry the heavy drum higher and after some
trial and error he found a branch that divided and gave a
delicately balanced lodgement for the drum.

He looked around. 'Was there some string or thin wire
with it?' he asked.

'There was monofilament fishing line through the handle,'
Jane said.

'Could you still find it?'

'I could try.' Jane sighed and got to her feet again. Roland
offered to go but Jane pointed out that he would not have
the faintest idea where to look. She set off and was soon
out of sight.

'Look out, below,' Ronnie called and he began to decant

water, a cupful at a time. 'Have a look downstream,' he told
Roland. 'There should be another length of fishing line. Try
the bank this side and any snags in the water. It'll be thin
stuff, hard to see, almost invisible if it's in the water. Feel
for it with your toes.'

Roland might not fully understand but he was beginning
to sense where Ronnie was going. He sat down and removed
his damp shoes and socks, placed them where they would
get the benefit of the sun and the light breeze to dry them,
rolled up his trouser cuffs and set about his search. A
minute's thought satisfied him that Ronnie was right. What
may be difficult to see may be more easily felt. He searched
until he found a detached stick among the twigs at the foot
of the tree. It was far from ideal but it would serve. The
stream soon widened, its pace slowed and he took to the
water, wading while feeling with his toes and with the stick.
He moved with care. The bottom was mostly sandy but
there were sharp stones among the sand and there might
even be broken glass. About a hundred yards downstream
a cluster of stones showed above the broken surface. He
prodded in that direction with his stick, but out of the corner
of his eye he saw the disturbance of a line of grass on the
bank. He climbed out. Running his stick through the grass
produced the disturbance again. The fishing line, when he
found it, was almost as invisible in the grass as it had been
in the water. It had several tangles in its length and it had
managed to twine itself among and around grass and nettles.

He was startled to find Jane towering over him. 'Ronnie
says to bring it just as it is without adding any more tangles
or pulling any of them tight. He had some rolled-up carrier
bags in his poacher's pocket, which is why his bum was
sticking out the way it was. He says to put each tangle into
a different bag and bring it to him like that.'

'You'd better help me separate it from grass and twigs,'
Roland said. 'How would he know that it would be tangled
liked this?'

Jane produced several carrier bags brightly printed with
the insignia of local firms, got down on her knees and began
work. 'Nylon monofilament always does tangle like this,

especially this light stuff, much thinner than what was on
the oil drum. It's one of the inescapable facts of an angler's
life. The heavier line that was on the drum was intended
to carry the weight of the drum, he says, but the light line
only had to act as a trigger.'

Roland had thought that he was beginning to understand
the country and its ways but this changed his mind for him.
'How did it happen that some of it was on the bank and
some in the water?'

'You're full of questions, aren't you? I'd say that it was
probably in the water and some creature walked or swam
into it and then walked ashore.' She saw Roland glance
around. The stream, sparkling on its way, seemed to have
a life of its own and yet showed no sign of other life. 'You
won't see much activity just now, we've scared most of it
underground or away. But try coming out here and sitting
very quietly at dusk and you'll be amazed. Ducks.
Moorhens. Water voles. Deer. Mink. Water rats. I could go
on.'

'Please don't bother,' Roland said.

Bearing three carrier bags containing a mixture of tangled
nylon and weeds, they arrived back at the bridge. Ronnie,
it seemed, had had time to conclude his other researches
and was seated on one of the boulders. He fumbled delicately through two of the carrier bags until he found a knot
in the nylon. 'It's been made into a loop. This is how it
could have been done,' he said. 'In fact, I'm damn sure it
was done. You want to see how?'

'Yes,' said the others. 'Of course we do,' Jane said.

'Right. Stand away from the wee knot in the timber of
the bridge where there was once a branch – that's about
where the danger will be. There's a knot – the other kind
of knot – that you can tie in monofilament. It's not well
known because it does just what you don't usually want
– it holds fast while there's a load on it and then lets go
as soon as it's slacked off. Now watch.' He touched the
oil drum with a gnarled finger. He had reduced the weight
of water in it until it took only a tiny tilt to allow the
water inside to shift the balance. The drum toppled and

began to fall. The supporting nylon was next thing to invisible against the broken background but, as with all fishing line, it was very much stronger than it looked. The drum swung in an arc that passed over the knot, about chest-high. As it rose on the continuation of the swing, it slowed and the tension grew less until suddenly it fell free and splashed into the water.

'Don't let it float away,' Ronnie said. 'It's evidence.'

Roland had begun to resume his now dried socks and shoes. He bared his feet again and waded after the drum.

'That looks horribly convincing,' Jane said in a choked voice. 'It could have knocked him off the bridge and down into the water. But there must have been something to spring the trap.'

'Aye, there is. That's why I had His Nibs there look for another length of nylon. It's a pity it's so fankled up you can't tell the length of it, but I'll unscramble it tonight.' Ronnie heaved himself to his feet. Roland was in no doubt that his exercise in the tree had tired the older man and irritated his joints.

Ronnie looked up into the branches, assessing angles. 'There must have been an anchorage point somewhere along here.' He began to search through the weeds beside the path opposite the roots of the tree. 'Maybe something natural or maybe something like a tent peg. Hah!' He parted the grass to show the base of a seedling tree, no more than an inch thick, that had been cut off a hand's breadth above ground. It had been given a notch, just like the tent peg that Ronnie had suggested. He shifted his attention to the other side of the path and found a root with a gap beneath where the ground level had sunk or been eroded by rain or traffic on the path. He went down on his knees, raising his imposing buttocks to the air, while he inspected the surface of the root. 'Thought so,' he said at last. 'Like a cut made by a blunt knife. The nylon went under here and up . . .' He paused, looking into the branches. 'My guess would be . . .' He lowered his eyes to Roland. 'Where's yon stick you were using?'

'I'll fetch it.' Fetching sticks, Roland felt, was more a

job for his dog but he carried out the errand anyway. Luckily he remembered where he had tossed it aside. Ronnie studied the surface. 'Look,' he said. Sure enough there were two thin dents in the bark at one end. At the other, and on the reverse side, there were marks that Roland could not interpret.

'My guess,' Ronnie said, 'would be that he ran the nylon under that root and up towards the drum. He took this stick, passed it through the loop of the nylon and then put it over the branch that the drum was sitting on and under the drum. Any pull like somebody walking into that nylon and the stick would tip the drum over, the stick would fall out and the nylon line would fetch up in the water. Or it would get hung up in the branches of the tree and if anyone ever noticed it they'd think that some angler trying for a trout had made a mess of his cast.'

'But,' said Jane. 'There's always a but. This particular but is that whoever it was couldn't just set the trap and walk away. Anybody could have walked into it. *I* could have walked into it. He'd have had to lurk, ready to distract the wrong person if they came along before GG did. Unlikely, I admit, but it could have happened. He could be in enough trouble without killing the wrong person. Well, he couldn't hide in the tree – Mrs Cadwallader spotted Ronnie straight away.'

'Looking down from up there,' Ronnie said, 'I could see where he'd have hidden. There's a deep hole among the boulders.'

Jane gasped. 'So there is!' she exclaimed. 'We found it, years and years ago, and forgot about it again, but we hid in it once and jumped out on somebody crossing the bridge, hoping that we'd make him fall in, but it didn't work that way and GG gave us a right old talking-to.'

'And serve you right.'

There was silence for a minute while each of them thought over the scenario. 'I buy it,' Roland said at last. 'In fact, I more than buy it. Add together the lengths of nylon, the marks in the bark, the cutting of that root, the stick and the oil drum. Take all those things together and you'd be demanding an impossible series of coincidences to explain them any other way.'

Jane's face had blanched. 'I agree,' she said. 'But that only drives home the point that somebody really did lay a trap for my great-grandfather and . . . and killed him. Now part of me wants to bury my head in the sand and pretend that I know nothing. The other part wants to see whoever harmed GG brought to justice, or as near to justice as the justice system ever manages, which isn't very close. I'd like to see him hanged or burnt at the stake; but even if he's convicted I suppose the sentence will be eroded by one factor or another until he's out and about again before he's even learned his way to the governor's office.'

'So what next?' Ronnie asked. 'The police?'

'I don't know,' Jane said slowly. 'Roland, will you go on helping me?'

Roland looked into her eyes which were colder than any ice. She was in a mood that could lead her into drastic action. It would be his duty to make sure that the police were informed, whether or not that was what she wanted. But if he did his duty she would never forgive him. If he refused her, God knew what she might not do. At least he must stay in touch. The words came out before he was ready for them. 'You know I will, not that I've been much help so far.'

Jane hesitated, opened her mouth and closed it again before turning to Ronnie. 'I'm very grateful and I'll write to Mrs Ilwand and say so. You've been brilliant. Now will you do me one more favour, a big one?'

'A'course I will.'

'Then forget all about this unless and until I say so.'

Ronnie hesitated. 'If there's more to be done, you'll not leave me out?'

'No, I won't do that.'

'You'll be needing your wee camera back, to show the police.' He handed over the camera. 'And I'll tell you one more thing. Whoever tied those knots wasn't a fisherman; they were no kind of knots for nylon. He's lucky they didn't slip.'

'Then how would he know how to tie a knot that would definitely slip when he wanted it to?' Roland asked.

Ronnie shrugged. 'If there was any knot left to look at I could maybe tell you. Lorry drivers and farmers have a knot that they use to tie down tarpaulins, that's the best I can think of.' He stepped back, nodded and turned away. He was walking very stiffly. Roland found it difficult to believe that the same man had been scrambling about in the branches of the tree, but when he said so to Jane she only remarked huskily that she had seen the same miraculous improvement in an elderly gundog at the sound of a shotgun closing or a beater's voice. She leaned her face against Roland's shoulder for a moment but when he moved to put a comforting arm around her she jumped away.

Roland looked back almost nostalgically as they moved. For him, the place did not have the connotation of the death of a loved one as it did for Jane. Instead, he had suddenly and for the first time caught a glimpse of the beauty that nature could achieve without man's help or interference. In his mind the writer's habit had taken over and he was searching for words to evoke sunshine dappled through leaves and playing over the ripples of a stream.

SEVEN

Morning had gone and half the afternoon with it before they were back at Jane's doorstep. 'These poor damn dogs,' she said. 'They're long overdue for a walk.'

'And I'm long overdue for soup and a sandwich. I wouldn't be leaving either of them to bust,' Roland pointed out reasonably. 'After all, they've had access to the gardens.' His objection was half-hearted. The day had turned out to be sunny without being too hot and he did not feel like confronting a blank screen.

'True though that may be,' Jane said severely, 'when you take on responsibility for a dog, the dog comes first.' She relented. 'You can take them both for a walk and I'll have something waiting for you when you come back. Here's King Coal's lead.'

An hour later, while they were in Jane's kitchen and finishing the mid-afternoon snack that they both knew would turn into a mere appetizer for the evening meal, Roland said, 'Well, assuming that the What and How have been solved, provisionally, next comes Who. But at this point I suggest that you turn to the police. They have facilities. They have people. And they have or can get power to compel answers. We have none of those things. Call to their attention the facts we now have that they didn't and sit back. They'll be duty bound to take over.'

Jane hesitated and then shook her head. 'Not yet. Most of the people around here are my friends. If I set the police on them, they soon won't be. I want to know a little more before I take a step I can't step back from and I want to be at the point where the immediate next step is an arrest. That way won't leave a long period of harassment while they all hate me. Bear with me for a little longer.'

'Might that be so that I can face the wrath of your friends and leave you still bright and shining?'

Jane bit back a furious retort. She would need Roland's goodwill later. 'I hadn't thought of that, but it's an idea. Please, Roland. Humour me.'

Roland had matters of his own demanding attention but he had a lot to learn about life outside the city and Jane was the person to teach it to him. He was about to give in, though with a dozen mental reservations, when a long peal on the doorbell coincided with a thunderous knocking. It caught Jane with her mouth full. Roland interpreted her gestures correctly and went to the door. The man waiting outside, without showing any signs of patience, was of medium height but lean and rather swarthy with a thin moustache. He was spattered with blood. 'Is the vet in?' he demanded hoarsely.

'Yes, but—'

The man turned, nodded violently towards a dilapidated van at the kerb and then hastened in the same direction. The rear door was flung open, another and fatter man emerged and the two men lifted out a bloodstained blanket. Before its owner could cover it with another blanket, Roland saw that it held a large and fierce-looking dog of mixed breeding. Even as a city-dweller, Roland had become well acquainted with the breeds encountered while chatting up girls in the park and this one, he thought, most resembled a Staffordshire bull terrier. The dog was obviously injured although how badly Roland was not qualified to say. It certainly seemed too sorry for itself to pose any threat.

He darted back to the kitchen. 'Two men coming with injured dog,' he said.

Jane threw up her hands and produced a gusty sigh. She folded the tablecloth off the table, uncovering neat tiles beneath. 'That will be Bart Hepworth, with his brother and Crippen,' she said. 'They'd better come in. You can go home, Roland, if you don't like the sight of blood. Or wait in the sitting room.' She cleared the dishes into the sink, removed the tablecloth and began to wipe the tiled surface of the table with a cloth and an antiseptic solution.

Roland and the other Mr Hepworth, each feeling *de trop,* adjourned to Jane's small sitting room. Hepworth felt a need for conversation and a disjointed discussion of the weather ensued. Hepworth, Roland decided, was an unintelligent man, sadly lacking education and whose mind was else-where. 'What happened to Crippen?' Roland asked suddenly.

The other shrugged. 'He got into a fight. Dogs do.'

'And he lost.' It would have taken a remarkable dog to get the better of the redoubtable Crippen when back on form. The scales fell from Roland's eyes. They were replaced by an idea, almost an inspiration. He decided to approach his subject very delicately and in a roundabout way. 'You were lucky to catch us in,' he said. 'We've just been visiting the place where Jane's great-grandfather died. You heard about that?' (He was accorded a nod.) 'Jane's very worried. The sheriff recorded a verdict of misadventure but the facts as given to the inquiry sounded quite unlike her great-grandfather as she knew him. Did you ever meet the old gentleman?' (A headshake.) 'He died from a fall into the stream from the log bridge just beyond his house from here. It seems to be quite a popular place for dog walkers and courting couples, but there's not the least trace of a witness. And yet I would have a bet that fifty people witnessed your dogfight.'

A blank expression wiped over Hepworth's face. 'Here! What are you getting at?'

'Jane has been helpful to your brother – more than once, from what she said. Now she could do with some help. You must know many dog owners and other men who are out and about at dusk and into darkness. Ask around for anybody who was near Whinmount on the night when Luke Grant died.'

'And why would I want to do that?'

His background had given Roland the habit of listening to what was really being said. 'You may not want to do it,' he answered. 'But you'll do it if you don't want your names mentioned to the police and the SSPCA in connection with illegal dog fighting. I have the strongest objections to it. Frankly, I'm surprised that Jane connives at it.'

Mr Hepworth sneered. 'Well, Mr Clever, if connive means what I think it means, she reads Bart a lecture every time he comes to her, but she likes the money and it's not in her to let a dog suffer. You think she'll thank you for clyping? You could get her into deep trouble. You could get her struck off.'

That was a real danger. Each of them had to know that Roland was bluffing. He stumbled on. 'This is me talking, not Jane. Find me somebody who was near Whinmount that evening and we'll say no more about it.'

For what seemed an hour but was probably little more than half that time, they sat and glared at each other between intervals of argument that flared and spluttered like a damp log on a bonfire. At last Jane came in, freshly washed but with traces of blood spatter. 'I've stitched him up, Ossie,' she told Hepworth. 'I think he'll do. He'll still need to be carried until the anaesthetic wears off. Bart wants you to go and help him.'

Ossie Hepworth had got to his feet but before leaving the room he confronted Jane. 'This bugger's talking about telling the fuzz about you-know-what.'

Immediately, Roland felt guilty. 'Only if he wouldn't help to find witnesses to the night your great-granddad died,' he said.

'Good idea!' Jane said.

'You wouldn't!'

'No, of course I wouldn't. I promised. And I couldn't, without admitting that I'd committed an offence. But I'm a little more subtle than that. If we don't get any help, the next time Bart brings a dog to me I'll refer him to the SSPCA and we'll see how he likes it. One good turn deserves another.'

'And vice versa,' said Roland.

The somnolent Crippen was carried out in sullen silence. 'That was nasty. It had only just missed the jugular.' An equally subdued Jane led the way back into the kitchen and set about an energetic cleanup. 'Well?' she said.

'You know very well what I'm going to say.'

'Say it anyway and we'll clear the air.'

'Very well,' said Roland. 'I've only known you a few days but I thought I knew you better than that. You're a professional animal carer. You seem to love dogs. How can you tolerate criminal dog fighting?'

Jane tossed the bloodstained cloth into the sink and sat down, locking eyes with Roland. 'I don't tolerate it. You didn't hear what I said to Bart but I saw him flinch. I think I touched a nerve. I certainly surprised myself with my own eloquence. I don't suppose it'll make any difference in the long run, but at least it's the most I can do and still treat the injured. What do you suppose would happen if I refused to help?'

'They'd have to find somebody else.'

'There isn't anybody else. Vets already in practice have too much to lose. So have I, but I need the money so badly that it has to be worth the risk. And if I didn't do it the owners would try to do it themselves in far from sterile conditions, cause a lot more suffering and probably end up killing the dog. Cheer up. I'll take you out to dinner tonight, with wine. Not the hotel and only the house red, but out all the same.'

Roland was relieved to find that they were still on good terms but he was happy to put off dining out until any tension on his own part had relaxed. 'Not tonight,' he said. 'I have to read text for your friend Simon Parbitter. His publisher's sending him angry emails.'

'So cheer up even more. We'll both be in funds. Maybe we'll be able to afford the hotel after all. When can we meet to start the Who list?'

'You'd better give me a day or two.' He began to get up but changed his mind. A complete irrelevancy had been teasing him. 'Why on earth is Ossie called that? Ozzie would have been Oswald, but Ossie?'

She sighed in the manner of somebody much put upon although she was in fact grateful for the partial change of subject. 'If you must know, it's short for Osfa.'

'Let's start again. Why on earth was Ossie named Osfa?'

'How would I know a thing like that?'

'You know all right,' Roland said. 'I saw your face change.

It took you a second to remember and then you looked amused.'

They were both relieved to have left the other topic behind. 'Persistent!' Jane said. 'It stands for One Size Fits All. And don't bother asking how on earth he got a nickname like that. I did hear the story, but it's not one that a young lady could repeat to a gentleman.'

Roland laughed without amusement. 'When did I qualify as a gentleman?' he demanded. 'Come on. You can tell me.'

Jane smiled. 'All right, I'll tell you. You're the first man who didn't make a pass when I cried on his shoulder. That's when you qualified as a gentleman.'

'I wasn't talking about that and you knew it.'

'I am bound by my oath of medical confidentiality,' she said with dignity.

'Does that apply to animals?'

'Probably.'

'But we're not talking about animals. We're talking about how one of your least reputable clients came by his nickname.'

'Think about it,' she said. 'You ought to be able to figure it out.'

EIGHT

I t happened that for several successive days Roland was engaged with Simon Parbitter's editing while Jane was called on to take blood samples from a herd of cattle for brucellosis testing. It was the following Friday before they were both free. Flush, for the moment, with funds, they agreed to enjoy their dinner together quickly, before the money was wasted on necessities. They were determined to make the most of the occasion, savouring life as it should be and as each remembered it from the good old days, as seen in the afterglow of retrospect.

A driving licence is essential to a vet so Jane was not going to put hers at risk. Her car was not insured for Roland to drive. Though extravagance was going to be the order of the day it would be canny extravagance. Dressed in what remained of their 'best' (Jane called it their 'least worst') they enjoyed a glass of elderflower champagne apiece before walking down through the 'green belt', over the canal and into the town. Instead of the hotel, they had booked a table in Giuliani's Bistro. An earlier visit with her great-grandfather had taught Jane that the best value in Italian wine was the Sangiovesi, so they shared a bottle and then another. They talked until suddenly the last of the daylight had faded. They split the cost of the meal and tip and, as the final extravagance, phoned Ledbetter's for a taxi.

The taxi was driven by Jimmy Benton, an old friend of Jane's. Jimmy drove agricultural machinery of all sorts during the working day, but by means of evening and weekend taxi driving he was earning money which he saved towards the day of his intended marriage to another of Jane's former school friends, now a student nurse at the cottage hospital. This provided sufficient topics of conversation to last for half of the way up the hill. Then Jane said, 'You know about my great-grandfather's death, Jimmy? But of course you do. You brought at least one party to the funeral. What are people saying about him now?'

'That he was a fine old chap and that it's a damn shame that he couldn't have gone on and seen his hundred. He used to say that if he didn't get a telegram from the queen, he wouldn't send her one.'

'Nothing else?'

'They say that you're not satisfied that it was an accident and that you're asking questions about it.'

'Who was saying that?' Jane asked sharply.

'Don't remember.'

'If you remember, or if anyone else says it, give me a ring.' They were nearing the hairpin bend where the farm road past Whinmount came off. At the last moment Jane said, 'Take us to my old home, Jimmy. Drive a little way past.'

'Righty-ho.'

'The taxi's my treat,' Jane whispered, sensing emanations of disquiet. They stepped out into brilliant moonlight. Jane fumbled in her purse for the right coins. As the taxi drove off, Roland said, 'If you felt the need for a walk we could have saved some money.'

Jane turned him and led him away from home. 'It's an easy walk on the level from here,' she said. 'I didn't fancy the pull up that hill one damn bit. I want to show you something and the only people we might meet at this time of night are dog walkers, which may even be useful.'

They linked arms. They had both become unused to alcohol and although they were speaking and even thinking clearly they welcomed the steadying support. She steered them past the cedar tree and the bridge. They crested the rise beyond. Jane's customary morning walk would have taken them into the woodland on their right but they passed that track and took to a later one that climbed along the edge of the trees through the resinous smell of pines. They stumbled occasionally over roots in the shadowed dark. It was a source of annoyance to Roland that Jane could hear the bats squeaking but he could not.

'I thought you'd taken a scunner to hill-climbing.'

'Not this one. I want to show you where some of the people live who GG knew best.'

'Remind me what sort of person we're looking for.'

Jane got a grip on herself. While the exercise was academic she could ignore the implications but now and again she was forced to accept that they were trying to seek out a real person who had committed a real act of aggression against her real and very dear great-grandfather. 'The person we want will be familiar with GG's habits, so probably a friend or a dog walker. That doesn't mean that I know him. GG often walked King Coal this way but he almost never introduced anybody who he met over here to his family – there was some sort of tension. He or she or somebody who owes him or her favours will be physically active enough to scramble about in the tree. Mechanically ingenious to be able to rig such a trap. He must have been out and about before GG that night and probably afterwards as well, to tidy up any leftover clues. He had some reason, real or imagined, to want GG . . . out of the way. That's all I can think of for the moment, except that he or she may not fit all those – what shall I call them?'

'Call them parameters. I don't know what it means in mathematics but in the real world I think it fills the bill.'

'Right. The person we want may not fit all those parameters but might have an accomplice to do the difficult bits.' Jane paused to draw breath but Roland seemed to manage the climb without difficulty. She supposed that her more sedentary student years had given him a start in the fitness stakes. This she found surprising. She thought that a vet's life involved more activity than that of a writer. Later, she discovered that it was his habit, whenever he needed thinking time, to go for a walk or a jog. 'Just as an off-the-top-of-the-head frinstance, I can't see Mrs Cadwallader swinging around in the branches but she has a son who seems to jump whenever she cracks the whip.'

'You're carefully avoiding mention of your sister and her husband.' He felt her jump. 'I suspect that they fit the parameters perfectly. And your voice changes slightly when you mention your brother-in-law. You don't think he could be to blame but you'd like it to be him, wouldn't you?'

There was a pause before Jane said, in a very small voice, 'Only if he really is guilty.'

Roland had checked in his stride but now he moved on. 'All right,' he said. 'When you're ready to tell me, I'll listen.'

The view opened up. Under the moon, the pattern of woods and fields showed up clearly. The landscape was mostly dark with here and there a spark of light drawing the eye to where a dwelling must be hiding in the gloom. The nearer and brighter lights formed a hollow square. Further off, Roland saw only a distant sprinkle of glints.

'There's a fallen tree somewhere just along here,' Jane said, 'that makes a good seat if you're not too worried about your clothes.'

'How I wish I still had clothes worth worrying about!'

'Then it's about time that you and I went shopping, next time there's anything in the kitty. You know,' Jane said reflectively, 'seen through the bottom of a glass, as they say, it's less difficult to visualize somebody having a real or imagined reason to harm poor GG. He was such a nice, well-meaning, benevolent – is that the same thing?'

'Yes,' Roland said. 'Literally.' He could hear the smile in his own voice.

'Here's the fallen tree. Don't laugh at me. I know precisely what I mean. What I mean is that it's not only bad people who get murdered. Good people can be simply infuriating. I'm sure more Christians than criminals got thrown to the lions.'

'I believe history supports that view,' Roland said. He groped for a comfortable seat on the tree trunk. 'Nothing can be more annoying than an attitude of holier-than-thou. But you were going to tell me who lives down there.'

'I still am,' Jane said with dignity. 'Where those nearest lights are used to be Wedell Farm. It's on very stony ground, only useful for pasture, so nowadays the land's grazed by two neighbouring farmers. GG never mixed much with the farmers except to buy meat or vegetables off them.

'The buildings at Wedell were converted into dwellings. The far side from here is the original farmhouse, extended into what used to be a small barn. The conversion was cleverly done. It's beautiful inside and it looks south into the courtyard which is garden and supposed to be looked after communally. Ross Grant lives there with Sheila. I believe he's some kind of an art historian. He was a relative of GG, which I suppose makes him a sort of cousin of mine, umpty times removed. We haven't paid each other much attention. Digging in the dimmest recesses of my memory I think that that may have been the man who passed us near the bridge, the thin man with silver hair. There had been some sort of coldness in the family and I didn't set eyes on him for years but GG used to visit with him occasionally. Ross's wife, Sheila, was very pally with my stepmother but I haven't seen her in ages. They have two sons and a daughter but the sons are married and usually away from home. I was at school with the daughter. She was all right but a bit of a suet pudding really. Thinking about it, I'm becoming more sure that that the man who passed us while we were looking at the bridge was him. Or he,' she added quickly, recalling Roland's English degree. 'Ross, I mean.

'To the east – the right as we look at it – is Mrs Cadwallader, who you've seen or at least heard and glimpsed. She lives with a housekeeper-cum-companion and the house is much too big for them. Mrs Cadwallader's either widowed or divorced or possibly separated, nobody seems very sure and one doesn't like to ask. GG tried to avoid her but she was always making up to him after my stepmother died. There had maybe been something between them about the time of Robert the Bruce. She has a hockey-playing daughter who's moved in with a shopkeeper in Kelso without benefit of clergy, and the word is that you only have to mention the daughter if you want to send Mrs Cadwallader on her way with her tail between her legs.

'In Wester Wedell, to our left, there's a gamekeeper named Holmes. The house is small because the main archway entrance to the central courtyard comes off it, but he's single so I suppose that's all right. Actually, it would make a lot of sense if he swapped houses with Mrs Cadwallader, because he does a whole lot of things like taxidermy and he stores a lot of materials for his keepering, but she thinks he's a bloody-minded sadist and he things she's a pissy-minded old bitch – well, that's what he called her – so the chances of them agreeing a swap are nil. Also he has a very well-trained dog which she's sure will eat her poodle some day. Anyway, she thinks that having the larger house lends her status. If GG walked this way, as he often did, Mr Holmes is who he'd usually visit.

'This side, there's a family called Adamson. They must be very affectionate or Catholics or something because she's one of the ugliest women I've ever seen and yet they seem to produce at least a baby a year. All those young children running around wild, leaving tricycles in the flowerbeds and toy cars on the paths, are not appreciated by the others, who are looking for peace and quiet and trying to keep the place tidy. He teaches at the school here but he also lectures at Edinburgh University so we don't see much of him. I believe he's some kind of a historian. I met him once. I did not like him.'

They sat in silence for some minutes. The temperature was falling and he felt her shiver. 'You're cold,' he said. He put an arm round her,

'That really is better,' she said. She sounded surprised. 'But this is only for warmth, remember.'

Roland had had time to think. 'We've reached a point where we have to decide. Either we go on enquiring, which has to mean asking people questions. Or we invoke the police. Either of those options means bringing your doubts and suspicions into the open. Or we can let it drop.'

'I'll think about it,' she said. 'For the moment, I'm getting cold again. Let's start back.'

They got up and started to walk. He steadied her with the arm round her waist but she knew the path and undertook the steering. They seemed to manage quite well. 'No more talking,' she said. 'I'd have heard if anyone was coming while we were sitting down, but now we don't know what ears are hidden in the darkness.'

They walked in silence, each taking comfort from the close contact. As they passed the lights of Whinmount their clasps tightened for a dozen paces. Soon they were among the street lights of Birchgrove. At Jane's gate, they paused. 'You can come in if you like,' she said very softly. It was late and neighbours would be lying abed and waiting for sleep to come. 'For brandy or a cup of Ovaltine or something.'

'Do you, in fact, have any brandy?'

'No. But that needn't stop you coming in for it.'

'True. I'll settle for a cup of tea or decaff coffee. A hot drink helps me to sleep but caffeine sees me wide awake.'

They settled in her small sitting room with mugs of tea. The room was different in dim light and with drawn curtains, definitely more feminine – but that, he thought, was probably a residue from the late step-great-grandmother. Jane took a seat on the settee and it seemed only polite to join her. 'Well, that was a jolly good evening,' she said. 'But we'd better not do it too often until our finances are more stable. We seem to be adequately provided with meat for the moment, but I thought of going fishing soon. GG gave me a year's subscription to the angling club for Christmas and I can take a guest.'

Roland's mind was not on food. 'It was your brother-in-law who –' He paused to choose his next words. *Broke your heart* was too sentimental and suited to a women's magazine. '– *treated you badly*,' he resumed. 'Wasn't it?'

On the point of telling him that it was none of his damn business, she remembered that he had been frank about his betrayal by the horrible girlfriend, whatever her name was. 'Yes,' she admitted. Her voice became almost inaudible. 'It was much the same story as yours except the other way round and he didn't pinch my money, but only because I didn't have any, I suspect. I think he was making hay with my sister at the same time. I think he'd decided that he was on a good thing. He was engaged to me first. Then he broke it off and he got engaged to my sister, but he was promising on everything he held sacred – you wouldn't believe the list of things he said he held sacred – to break it off with her and to marry me. And I believed him.' She paused. Would he think less of her if she admitted the full extent of her folly? It was different for a man, but at least he had been honest with her. 'On one occasion he got straight out of my bed and into hers. I must have been mad. What hurts is that I think she knew all along and thought that it was funny.'

She waited to see whether Roland showed signs of shock but his mind was deeper into the human relationships. 'I wouldn't be too sure about that,' Roland said. 'It's a normal human instinct in times of disaster to think that others are laughing at you but usually they aren't.'

'She more or less admitted it. That's why I had to get out of the house.' She turned her face away to hide her tears.

Roland was truly shocked except that a tiny part of his mind was registering the story and considering the effect of its possible inclusion in a novel. It would make a good motive for a murder, the story to emerge slowly during the investigation. 'I think that that's the lousiest, most despicable trick that I ever heard! How did GG react?'

'He was not pleased. Not one damn bit. And he didn't even know the whole story.'

'And this was how long before he died?'

'Just a few weeks. Do you think—?'

'I think you may get your wish. Isn't it possible that your GG was angry enough to threaten to change his will?'

'I suppose it's possible,' she said. 'You'd better make a note of it. Well, one good thing, at least I made damn sure that I didn't get pregnant.'

She had more to say but she broke off, watching him out of the corner of her eye. It might be a mistake to remind him about sex, but he did not look shocked. Instead, he pulled her to him. He wanted to find words to express his sympathy and to apologize on behalf of the whole human race but the words were slow to come. When he saw her tears, he began to kiss them away, one at a time. She offered her lips and for a moment they kissed. Then she pushed him away. 'I'm sorry,' she said, 'but no. Not yet. It wouldn't be appropriate.'

'Why not?'

'I can't explain. It just wouldn't. I think you should go home now.' She managed to control her breathing until he was out of the room.

NINE

Roland was slow to fall asleep. He was uncertain whether he had damaged his relationship with Jane. When he woke again in the small hours the same worry was still with him, which he took for a sign, if one were needed, that his attitude was becoming more than brotherly. Jane also woke early, but her concern was that her admission that she had slept with her future brother-in-law might make him think of her as easy meat. Her opinion of men was at a low ebb.

The dogs had to wait, with the patience given to some of their species, for their walk that morning. Working dogs have an inbred aptitude to wait, knowing that the next call to work would be on the way soon enough. Each of their owners was waiting to see the other set off so that their encounter would obviously be accidental. In the end, Roland decided that she must have slipped out unobserved and he gave up the wait, only to meet Jane and King Coal at the first corner. With no more than an exchange of 'Hello', they fell into step. By common, tacit consent they headed in the familiar direction.

At first they said nothing. Roland was first to run out of patience. 'Last night, did I offend you?' he asked.

Jane felt a flood of relief. She had been tempted to ask the same question but hesitated to open a subject that might be better left closed. 'Not in the least,' she said. *Too heartily*, she told herself when it was too late.

'That's good. I was worried. But about the only piece of good advice that my father ever gave me was that no woman ever objects to being –' he hesitated. The word that his father had used was *desired*. '– admired,' he substituted.

Jane, while feeling that there might be some truth in the edict of Mr Fox Senior, decided that the conversation was heading in a direction that should definitely be avoided – for the moment. She let him see the red canvas training dummy in her hand. 'I was going to give King Coal a refresher,' she said. 'The grouse season will be around again shortly. He may be getting on but he can still do a day's work and they'll be crying out for reliable pickers-up because the keepers are all needed in the beating line and when it's a commercial shoot they're paid by the number of birds in the bag. The money's rubbish and they don't usually give you a brace of grouse as they would at the pheasants, but the tips are sometimes good. Has Sandy been trained to the gun?'

'That I can't tell you,' Roland admitted. 'A former colleague of mine was suddenly offered a good job in Malaysia and he couldn't take Sandy with him. I think he had been intending to shoot.'

'We'll try him and see,' Jane said. 'But we may be too late to get him up to scratch for this year.' They were passing a track that led up the hill to their right. 'That's the way that I usually go, but I think we might go on and give you a daylight look at Wedell. We might even call on Mr Holmes, if he's in. If he's at his release pens, they're only a step further on. He may be the best source of local gossip. He has the reputation of being a rude, evil-tempered bastard. GG was the one person he was pally with; on the other hand, he'd quarrelled with everybody else and it's surprising how much you find out about somebody in a good-going row. He can be a dour kind of creature. We'd have to see what sort of mood he was in.'

They crested the rise. 'Well, talk of the devil,' Jane said.

An olive-green Land Rover pickup had been stopped at the side of the road, if a road so narrow can be said to have sides. A drystone wall ran along the right-hand side of the road and beside it lay a dog, a German short-haired pointer. A man got up from kneeling beside the dog and said a few words to it. The dog relaxed visibly. He ran towards them, very clumsily in his heavy work boots.

'Mr Holmes?' Roland said. 'The keeper?'

'Yes.'

The keeper arrived, panting and sweating. He was wearing

jeans and a sweater too thick for the muggy day. There could be no doubt that he was thoroughly upset. He was a wiry man, weather-beaten, red-haired and possessed of a round face that nature had never intended to be cheerful and was now woebegone. Either his eyes were habitually watery or he was close to weeping. 'Miss Grant,' he gasped. 'Miss Highsmith, I should say. Thank God you're here. I was just about to load Dram into my truck and fetch him to you only I was feared to hurt him more. Come, please, quickly.' He turned away and pounded off back towards his dog. Roland and Jane jogged after him.

Dram, the GSP, was evidently suffering both pain and fear. Without interrupting his steady, low moan he raised his head and looked pleadingly at his master. When King Coal, out of no more than sympathetic curiosity, nosed the pointer, it gave a strangled yelp. Holmes made an involuntary movement with his foot.

Jane straightened quickly and confronted the keeper, nose to nose. 'Don't you dare!' Jane growled. 'Don't you lift your boot against my dog or I won't lift a finger to help yours. I thought you knew better than that. Now, calm down and tell me what happened.'

The keeper looked ready to explode but he went down on his knees to nurse the dog's head. 'I don't know exactly what the hell happened,' he said in a shaking voice. 'I'd finished my jobs at the rearing pens and I was heading home in the truck for my piece. I let Dram sprint across the grass – the exercise does him good and it's his one chance to go flat out. We have a kind of race between us and he always wins, which makes him feel good.'

The keeper's voice was half choked. His breathing was steadying but his hands, which were stroking the dog's head, still shook. Jane thought that he might be communicating his panic to the dog. On the other hand, the contact was comforting them both. She decided to let well alone. 'Go on,' she said.

'This time, I reached the front door and he just wasn't there. I thought maybe he'd got a whiff of a bitch in season. That'd be more than enough.' He glanced from Roland to

Jane but decided against making any remark. 'I looked across the field, back the way he usually comes. You get a better view from the higher ground and I saw him lying here, so I got back in the truck and followed him up. See this hole?' The keeper pointed to a deep hole half hidden in the grass and weeds between the wall and the road. 'They're putting in some drainage – this road floods something awful in winter. He must've jumped the dyke and landed half in the hole. I reckon his back's broke.' The keeper's voice was shaking worse than ever and there were tears running down his face. 'He tried to crawl to me – for a comfort I couldn't give him. I couldn't bear to see him suffering so. I wanted to go for my gun and put him out of it but when I tried to leave him he wanted to come after me and that hurt him so much that he cried out to me. Will you keep him quiet while I fetch my gun? Or will you take my truck and go for the stuff to . . . end it?'

'Calm down,' Jane snapped at him. 'You're not helping him at all.' Roland filed away in his mind the picture of the hardened keeper, broken by love of his dog, being faced down by the fresh-faced girl. Words to paint the picture were dancing through his mind.

'But—'

'It's not up to you to make that decision. No way would I put an animal down without an examination.'

'You'll not hurt him? I wouldn't want him hurt.'

'Nor would I. Just hold him steady and keep him as calm as you can.' Jane reached under the recumbent animal. Holmes flinched at every movement but the dog seemed to recognize that somebody who knew what they were doing was trying to help. After several minutes, Jane straightened. 'If I ever dislocate my back like this, get me into the Orthopaedic Department of the New Royal. I'll leave instructions that you're not to be allowed within a mile of me after that. Now, keep hold of his head. Your job is still to keep him as calm as you can and turn his head to keep it in line with the rest of his body. Roland, you take his chest and I'll take his hips and we'll very slowly turn him onto his back.'

Roland looked shocked. 'Wouldn't it be better if Mr Homes did that and I took the head?'

'Mr Holmes is too upset,' Jane said. 'You'll do all right. But listen, both of you. I don't think that he'll start to squirm but he might, in which case hold him tightly. Keep him as still and as straight as you possibly can.' Under her guidance, Dram was gently rolled onto his back. The other two dogs came closer and watched with interest. Jane spoke soothingly to Dram and rubbed his legs. Her hands stroked round his hips. Then she suddenly flicked the knees of his hind legs across. The dog squirmed for a moment and then seemed almost to relax. The quivering in his muscles stilled. Mr Holmes drew in a breath of terror, convinced that she had killed his dog.

Jane felt underneath and ran her fingers along his spine again. 'That's as good as we can make it for now. You'll have to keep him off his feet for days if not weeks but I think he'll make it all right in the end. No running and jumping, not that he'll want to. No more walking than he must do in order to go and do his business on the grass. If he has difficulty in supporting his own weight, help him or get a few friends to help you carry him. Now, do you have a blanket, a piece of tarpaulin, anything we can use as a stretcher?'

'I can let go of his head now?'

'Try it and see.'

Dram was settled enough. He lay limp as Holmes rose and fetched a groundsheet from his Land Rover. They laid it beside Dram and then, with great care, slid the anxious but compliant dog onto it.

Jane looked across the single pasture to where Wedell sat squarely under the sun on a rise of ground. The buildings were domestic in detail but still showed the shape of farm buildings. 'I have never had such a good patient,' she said, 'but I think that expecting him to accept being lifted into and out of your pickup and being bumped around in the back in between might be asking too much. I think we'll have to carry him.'

Jane and Roland took a front corner apiece and Holmes

took hold of the rear corners. With his master in sight and speaking soothingly, Dram settled in his unconventional hammock.

'Did they teach you that in Vet College?' Roland asked. 'Being an osteopath, I mean.'

'I spent my year out in the States, studying veterinary chiropractic,' Jane said. 'It seemed to be the one area my course hardly touched on and yet it was an obvious lack.'

'Is that the same as osteopathy?'

'Not quite. But similar.'

The distance to the Wedell houses had seemed to be no more than the length of a football field, but soon it felt closer to that of an eighteen-hole golf course. The way, which had looked almost level, soon proved to have an uphill slope that began to seem progressively steeper as they tired. Dram was lean but heavily muscled and large for a GSP, certainly no lightweight. They had dressed in expectation of a cooler day and Roland, for one, was soon sweating. Before they had gone a hundred yards there was no breath to spare for conversation. The converted farm buildings crept very slowly nearer.

Holmes, who was overdressed for the day and carrying half the dog's weight uphill, was soon running with sweat and, despite being obviously fit, he was gasping. From the colour of his fingers Roland guessed that he was a smoker. They were relieved by the sudden appearance of a woman, strongly built and strong featured yet at the same time feminine, who took the fourth corner of the groundsheet without a word as though it were the inevitable thing to do. Her dark red hair, darker than the keeper's, was cropped short but with style. She wore no make-up but Roland was aware of a faint trace of perfume.

At last they arrived at the keeper's door. The burden was laid down gently while the keeper opened a way through to his kitchen. The newcomer stooped once to give the recumbent dog a sympathetic pat. She was thanked – which she did not seem to expect – and made her departure. Only when Dram was comfortably disposed in his basket by the range were the others able to lower themselves into Windsor kitchen chairs and stretch their stiffened muscles.

'That was Miss James,' Jane said as she recovered her breath.

Holmes got up again to put the kettle on. 'Thank God you arrived in the nick of time,' he told Jane. His voice was shaking. 'But for you I'd have put him down. I was certain sure his back was broke and I couldn't bear to see him suffering the way he was. He's not just a dog to me. Best dog I ever had. Best friend. God, I'll miss him when he goes, but maybe he has a few years yet. He'll be all right now?'

'I think so. No promises, but I'll bring you in some medication to keep him relaxed and to help the healing process. Call me if there's any problem. I'll look in now and again anyway.' For some minutes she lectured the keeper on the treatment required by a convalescent dog.

Holmes made tea. They nursed heavy mugs. Jane glanced around. The kitchen was much as GG must have known it – a plain room but clean, simply furnished and tidy. If there was ever to be a propitious moment, this had to be it. 'I was coming to you in the hope of some information,' she said.

For a moment it was as though the keeper had real hackles and raising them was his habitual reaction when asked for a favour. But then he remembered that he was under an obligation. 'Go ahead,' he said warily.

'You knew my great-grandfather well, didn't you?'

'I suppose so.'

'He came here oftener than to anywhere else. What did you talk about?'

'Things.' Holmes felt that that did not quite cover the subject. 'Country things. He liked to be told about wild creatures, how they acted and why. He said it helped him to get his photographs real-looking.' The keeper began to rouse from his depression. 'And, by God, it worked for him! His photies were some of the best I ever saw. Anything from a deer to a dormouse, he could show it just ready to walk off the page and with every hair as sharp as a razor-cut. He was a clever man, your great-granddad, and a fine man too.'

'Did you often walk together?'

'What's that supposed to mean?'

Jane hid a sigh. The keeper was obviously poised to find a hostile meaning in the most innocent of words. 'Nothing,' she said, 'except that he's said to have fallen off the wee bridge near Whinmount. Did that surprise you?'

'Aye, it did that. He was old – he said sometimes that if he didn't get his telegram from the queen he wouldn't send her one – but damn! I'm half the age he was and yet he was as steady on his feet as I am. But this last year or two he maybe leaned on his stick a bittie more and if his stick slipped . . .'

Jane paused for thought, wondering how to bring the conversation back to a more productive subject. 'Did he have any other friends in Wedell?' she asked.

The keeper had used the brief lapse in the talk to kneel beside the dog's basket. It seemed that Dram had accepted his new status as a patient and had found a position that was as near as he could get to comfortable. He was now lying limp. When Holmes stooped over him he turned his head to lick his master's hand and, to his owner's delight and Jane's secret relief, his tail thumped twice. When Holmes returned to the table it was clear that his mood of affable loquacity had taken on fresh life. 'Not to say friends. If somebody spoke to him in a friendly way, he was aye ready to reply the same way and he'd stay friends until he was given reason to change, but I never saw him on more than nodding terms with any of the others hereabouts.

'Mrs Cadwallader, now, in Easter. Well, they were never what you'd call thick as thieves, but she was very friendly towards him and he'd never be less than gentlemanly to her. Until about a couple of years ago, that was. Just after your stepma died, there was a row. That didn't surprise me one damn bit – that's a woman I can't thole at any price. Mr Adamson, who lives next door, is a cousin of yours, isn't he?

'No. It's his neighbour Ross Grant who's related,' Jane said. 'He and Mr Adamson are friendly, I believe.'

'Well, I was walking back from the Canal Bar one evening and so was Adamson and we'd both had a dram or two so we fell to talking, the way one does, gossiping like two old wives. I gather he's some sort of historian and very interesting he made it sound. He doesn't travel around like he used to, except to give talks – the Internet, he said, made it unnecessary. Anyway, he reckoned that she'd had a fancy for Luke Grant for years but that your step-great-grandma had warned her off. So when she died – your step-great-grandma I mean – the old biddy decided to try her luck again and got told that she'd no chance. And from something he'd heard – Mr Adamson I mean – they'd maybe been more than friends a good few years ago and she wanted to pick up where they'd left off but he didn't fancy it. Couldn't blame him, really – he was a whole lot older than her but he wore his age with dignity while she was trying to pass herself off as being next thing to a teenager.'

'Took it badly, did she?' Roland asked.

'You could put it like that. Kept quiet about it, didn't she? But whenever his name came up she'd look as though someone had farted.' He broke off and looked at his watch. 'Christ! Look at the time! I'll have to go about my chores or they'll never be done, but what to do about Dram I don't know.'

'Lend me your Land Rover for five minutes,' said Jane. 'I'll dash home and fetch a painkiller that will let him sleep all afternoon.'

The keeper looked almost happy. He came out with her to give her the key. He lit a cigarette from a gas lighter, talking through the smoke with half-closed eyes. 'That's great,' he said. 'But how long before he can work again?'

'Weeks,' Jane said simply.

Roland had followed them outside. 'If I could make a suggestion,' he said, 'why don't you borrow Sandy for a while? He's had some training but I don't know how much.'

He had said so little that the other two showed surprise. 'Good idea!' Jane said. 'Mostly, you'd want a dog for dogging-in, which is easy-peasy. He's very biddable and he takes direction well. You could be teaching him steadiness at the same time. Get him ready to pick-up for Roland. In return, you feed him, that's all.'

The keeper tried hard to think of an objection, but failed. 'We'll give it a try,' he said.

TEN

The keeper, in a rare burst of consideration, offered them a lift back to Birchgrove but, for the sake of King Coal, Jane and Roland decided to walk. They set off on foot. Mr Holmes would keep Sandy for the day, returning him to Roland each evening if the arrangement proved satisfactory. Sandy, after a puzzled look to his owner for reassurance, settled down beside Dram.

When they reached the keeper's Land Rover, Jane got in and backed it into a field gate for the sake of any traffic to come. In the shadow of the drystone wall, mushrooms were growing. Jane filled one of the polythene bags that she always carried against such a gift of nature. They walked on. Roland said, 'It's a little early for mushrooms. You're quite sure that they're safe?'

'I wouldn't put myself at risk,' Jane said. 'These are safe; the weather brought them on early. Field mushrooms have pinkish undersides. The dangerous ones grow among trees; they're usually slimmer than proper mushrooms and the frills underneath are white. If you pick mushrooms and intend to eat them, show them to me first.'

Roland promised to do that. 'It's been an interesting morning so far, but tiring,' he said. 'I've seen you exhibit an unusual talent, I've found out about mushrooms and we've learned a little about Mrs Cadwallader. I don't want to be a bore but I still want to know when you're going to tell the police.'

'Soon,' Jane said. 'Quite soon now, when we have a little more to go on than Ronnie's opinion of the traces plus a few scraps of nylon fishing line. I know that Ian Fellowes, our local detective inspector, has some respect for Ronnie's talent as a tracker, but I'd like us to have some corroboration. I don't want to be brushed off as a mischief-maker and time-waster.'

'I don't think there's much danger of that, but you're the boss. Who do we see next?'

'Who do you think?'

Roland took a dozen paces before he replied. 'We'll have to find out who's been buying nylon line, but it needn't have been bought locally – or bought specially. Apart from that, we're beginning to see the questions to be asked but we don't have much idea of what sequence they should be asked in. The answer you get from one person should lead to another – probably back to the person you saw the day before yesterday. Let's just go on talking to people as and when they turn up. We may have to go round them again later.'

Jane laughed and then pulled a face. 'I can't quarrel with that. But I'd rather put off seeing my sister and her dear, dear husband until I feel a bit more aggressive.'

'You're surely not afraid of them? Not while I'm with you?'

'Not afraid,' Jane said, 'no. But I feel the need of a little extra moral stamina. I don't like rows and arguments and when they're within the family I really hate them. And the fight we had the last time I saw Violet was the one to end them all. It still hurts. It was as if she'd been resenting me for years and it all came boiling out and I still don't know what got up her nose. Violet and I were really close for years and years. We had our squabbles . . . I was just going to ask, rhetorically speaking, what siblings don't, but then I remembered that you wouldn't know about that.'

'I'm not totally ignorant,' Roland said with dignity. 'Literature is full of sibling bitterness. Cain and Abel. Cardelia, Goneril and Regan. Dozens of others but not so many examples of them killing each other. Whose side did GG take?'

'I don't know. The will hasn't been dealt with in detail yet. The executor is a solicitor, a one-man-band who's heavily committed to a case that began in a small way and just plain grew until it's ended up in the House of Lords with God knows how many senior counsel dipping their fingers in the pie. I'm told that it's about to finish, so our trivial affairs may get a little attention soon.'

They walked a dozen paces while Roland digested that news. Then he said, 'As soon as he's available, we should look into all aspects of that. Not just the legacies but who knew about—'

'Sh!' As they crested the hump Whinmount was making a slow appearance, starting from the topmost chimney pot and giving the creepers on the old stone walls the appearance of rapid growth. 'There's no sign of life,' Roland said.

Jane hurried the pace. 'I'm sure they're there,' she said. 'I can feel them.'

Just as they reached the house, what she had dreaded came about and the front door opened. The figure of Violet, slightly taller than her sister but otherwise remarkably similar, appeared on the doorstep. She was also perceptibly the older, Roland noticed. She was smartly dressed, though with due regard to the cooler weather, and carrying driving gloves. She turned in the direction of the concrete garage that had been a late addition by GG. Seeing Jane, she hesitated.

Jane was expecting bitter words but Violet smiled. It was, Roland thought, a difficult smile to interpret. Warmth only crept into it after the first instant had gone by. 'Jane! I hope you weren't going to walk by without paying us a call.'

'But you're going out,' Jane said. Her voice had gone husky.

'Only to the shops. Nothing that can't wait. Do come in. After all, you do have some sort of squatter's rights. And who's this?'

Jane drew Roland forward. 'This is Roland Fox. The novelist, you know,' she added grandly.

Violet was torn between a desire to take Jane down a peg or two, a half-hearted wish to heal any breach that might have developed between them and relief that Jane had found herself an almost presentable man at last. She greeted Roland politely without giving any clue as to whether or not she had ever heard of him. 'Do come in, both of you,' she said. 'The kettle's still hot. I'll make tea.'

'Please don't bother,' Jane said. 'I'll have to get home. I'm expecting a delivery.'

Violet noticed the singularity. 'Come for a meal tonight, then, sevenish. Both of you. You *are* together?'

In the context, there was no easy answer. Rather than embark on explanations, they thanked her and hurried away. A new-looking Mini passed them with a friendly toot before they reached the B-road.

'That takes care of this evening's meal,' Roland said. 'She didn't seem too formidable to me.'

'She was on her best behaviour. But you'll have the doubtful pleasure of meeting my brother-in-law.'

'Would you like me to beat him up for you?'

Jane kept a straight face. 'Could you?'

'I don't know. Could I?'

She looked at him speculatively. 'I don't know either.'

'Well, just remember that I offered.'

'You're my knight in slightly tatty armour. Get on your horse, fetch your least rusty armour and we'll give it a sponge and press while we decide what line to take tonight.'

While Jane was performing her renovation on what Roland, stealing both phrases from Jane, called his 'least worst bib and tucker', Mr Holmes arrived with Sandy. The keeper looked tired but the big retriever seemed to have enjoyed himself. He had been thoroughly brushed. Holmes reported that Dram had been up but seemed happy to limp back to his bed. He also said that Sandy's basic training had been well managed and that he had the makings of a good gundog. Then, shedding the last traces of his forceful manner and becoming what was, for him, almost grovelling, he admitted that, while he would be delighted to pay Jane for her services it might be some weeks before he would be in a position to do so.

'That,' Jane said, 'is all par for the course. Join the club. I know that a keeper's income depends largely on the tips that he gets during the coming season, which won't start until a very few hours before you settle up with me. Right?'

The keeper took a second or two to pick out the implication. 'Right,' he said.

'Don't you forget, now. I'm at the front of the queue with my tongue hanging out. Well, Mr Fox and I are in much the same positions, for different reasons. We are rather short of protein and we will soon be getting very tired of rabbit and pigeon meat. So here's where we can do a deal. You keep two or three pigs at that compound where you bring on your poults, right?'

The keeper settled in one of the kitchen chairs and put a finger to his lips. Evidently the existence of his pigs was not intended to be public knowledge. He prepared to negotiate. 'I was planning to kill Fatima soon. But I don't like killing my own pigs. I know them, you see, and they've come to trust me.'

The crusty keeper was showing signs of a soft centre but Jane remained businesslike. 'Never mind about not liking to kill your own pigs,' Jane said. 'The law doesn't allow you to do that any more.'

'Och, I don't pay heed to the likes of that. I'm away off the beaten track and the meat inspector doesn't know I've got them. Now, if you were to kill and butcher her for me I could let you have some choice meat as payment. If anyone asked, you could say that she'd fallen and broken her leg. You're a qualified vet. You'd be entitled to put her down.' When Jane hesitated he went on. 'I could aye break her leg to make it true.'

Roland, who would have run a mile from any such task, was expecting Jane to refuse indignantly. Jane was indeed perturbed, but at the suggestion of cruelty rather than the breach of the law as imposed by the nanny state. On the other hand, to kill the pig before any such brutality occurred would be to save it pain, which would be well within her obligations as a vet. Such convoluted thinking, she decided, would have to satisfy. 'No problem,' she said. 'I've done it all before. But which cuts, exactly, do I get to keep?'

Shortly after seven, the two arrived at the front door of Whinmount. Jane's discomfort at being obliged to ring the doorbell at what had been her home from birth until very recently was multiplied when the door was answered by her brother-in-law. Manfred Young was revealed to Roland as being taller than average but slightly gangling, in his early thirties, with a full head of carefully waved dark hair and a face that Roland considered to be excessively handsome. At that point, however, Roland was relieved to see that the other's face was slightly effeminate with a Cupid's bow for a mouth. He was stooped and distinctly hollow-chested. Roland's interest in avenging Jane's mistreatment revived, but they shook hands affably enough without any trial of strength, each perhaps recognizing a possible future relative by marriage or finding a common bond with another who had been saddled from birth with a risible first name. Roland's eagerness to avenge the slight to Jane abated when Manfred claimed to recognize his name as that of the author of *The Temptation,* although Roland suspected him of a quick dash to the public library when he heard of the invitation.

They were led into the sitting room. Jane was quick to notice that the furniture had been freshly covered and that their hostess had a new dress. Sounds and smells of cooking percolated from the kitchen. With Violet and Manfred in the sitting room mixing drinks and making conversation, that meant that help had been brought in. Finances must be looking up.

But perhaps they were not looking as high as all that. When Roland was sipping a large gin-and-tonic, Violet smiled at her sister. 'I suppose you're driving,' she said.

Jane returned the smile. 'We walked.' Violet gave her husband a look which Jane interpreted as meaning, *Not too strong and use the cheaper gin.* Those words would have been an accurate prescription for the drink that eventually reached her.

Violet was looking at her watch. 'We're expecting Ross Grant and Sheila,' she said. 'You remember Ross?'

'Vaguely,' Jane said. 'I haven't seen him for years, except that I think that we nodded to each other in passing the other day. I haven't seen Sheila since GG's funeral. Ross's father was some sort of cousin of GG's,' she explained to Roland. 'They live in Wedell. But they never socialized. Was there a falling-out?' she asked Violet.

'I think so, but I was only a teenager and you were

hardly out of the egg. GG never spoke about it and it didn't happen here, but Ross's family was never invited to this house again. Once or twice, when Ross's father was mentioned, GG looked put out; but I quite liked Ross himself and I don't think that GG had anything against him, so when GG died and Ross wrote a very nice letter of sympathy it was obviously time to let bygones be bygones. Do I hear a car?'

'There's a car coming,' Roland said, 'but it's coming from the direction of Birchgrove. If they live in Wedell—'

'They've probably been down in the town,' Jane explained, 'and there's no more direct road.'

When Ross and Sheila Grant made their entry, after a tedious fuss over where they might park and where to put their coats and what drink they could accept if one or other of them (still to be nominated) were driving the mile or two to Wedell, introductions were performed and they were settled with a small sherry apiece. Ross was confirmed as the man who had passed them in the road. He was a fussy little man, not old but silver-haired and walking with a stick that he seemed to use for balance rather than to support his weight. His wife was younger and, though becoming fat, was not yet obese. Unlike her husband, who was comfortable in a corduroy jacket and flannels, she had gone to some trouble with her appearance, even donning some modest jewellery. She had a faint moustache, however, that would have yielded to a wax treatment.

'I suppose dinner can wait a very few minutes more,' Violet said. Those few minutes were given over to strained conversation about nothing before Violet drove them ruthlessly into the dining room. As he walked with Jane through the freshly decorated hall Roland noticed that, although the company was sending out signals that he could only interpret as hostile, the house itself was steeped in an atmosphere of welcome. No matter who inhabited it, the house was friendly.

As Jane had supposed, the meal was served by Hannah Folsom. Hannah was a widow with several children and a dependent mother. She earned most of her family's income by going out to cook, ably but expensively, for special occasions. Hannah was no stranger to Whinmount. Before the advent of Mary, GG's second wife (who was another gifted cook), she had occasionally been invited to cater a meal for one or another of GG's ladies. Being plump, still quite pretty and ageless, she was sometimes rumoured to have been one of their number though this was negated by the total lack of jealousy that she showed when serving one of them at table.

While the soup was being enjoyed the conversation was mostly about local politics, in which Jane joined eagerly. When the main course, of poached salmon, was on the table and Hannah had withdrawn, Roland looked across the table to Sheila Grant. 'I believe you live in Wedell,' he said. 'Don't you find it rather lonely?'

She laughed. 'Heavens, no! It's worth any amount of isolation to have the peace and quiet and the beautiful and changing outlook. It's no distance into the town. We're neither of us great walkers any more, but if the day comes when we can't afford a car, even an electric one, we can count on the family for shopping or do our weekly shop by computer. If I want society, I'm very good friends with Hilary Adamson. And, of course, there are other households near Wedell which are only a cough and a spit away, if you'll forgive the expression.'

There was a hiccup in the talk as each person wondered whether to forgive the expression. Roland felt obliged to keep the conversation going and saw an opportunity to pry further. 'And you don't feel bored or isolated?'

'No again. Housekeeping's a great time filler. Ross still has his research and he's called on to lecture now and again. He's a historian, you know.'

Ross, who seemed to have lapsed into a reverie, woke up. 'History of Scottish Art,' he said, 'which brings me into contact with Hugh Adamson who also lives in Wedell. He's a historian of Scottish history generally. We bore each other half to death on the more abstruse subjects of Scottish Victorian art –' he transferred his eye contact to Violet '– but we have a common interest in your great-grandfather's grandfather, who was also mine less one generation. That was Wyvern Grant. He was quite famous in his day, you know.'

'No, I didn't know,' Violet said. She was relieved at the arrival of a subject in which she could at least pretend an interest. 'GG never spoke about family history older than himself. What was Wyvern famous for?'

'He was an artist, but with more talent for self-promotion than for art. During his lifetime he gained some slight reputation as a portrait painter. An unjustified reputation, because he was no more than a moderately competent draughtsman. A camera, if there had been such a thing, could have done the job better and more cheaply. Very few of his paintings still exist, which is a great pity for a different reason.' Ross, who had cleared his plate, seemed about to lean his elbows on the table but remembered his manners in time. The mantle of the habitual lecturer was on him. 'You see, he mingled with the other painters of his generation, the bad as well as the good. His diaries give a valuable insight into the artistic and other establishment of the time, although they also show his judgement of his peers to have been – let's just say – less than trustworthy. Also, he painted a number of second-rank celebrities of the time, and nobody else bothered to leave us a record of what they looked like – or their backgrounds, because he seems to have been meticulous about filling in the details of houses, furniture and trivia. According to more than one of his contemporaries he had several highly regrettable habits—'

He was interrupted by the removal of the plates, the arrival of the sweet course and the need to choose between lemon meringue pie and sticky toffee pudding. Roland, who loved to hear about the regrettable habits of the famous in the hope that one or more would trigger a fresh novel, would have returned to the subject except that Jane was being put through an interrogation and he felt obliged to come to her aid.

'Don't you think,' Violet asked her sister coldly, 'that before stirring up a lot of mud around GG's death you might have consulted others of the family?' Roland guessed that this had been one of the principal objectives of the gathering.

'You are the only close blood relative I have left,' Jane said, thus excluding the others from any entitlement to be consulted. 'You had already announced that you were perfectly satisfied with the fiscal's interpretation.'

'Jane has been trying very hard *not* to stir up any mud,' Roland said.

'And how do you come into it?' Violet asked sharply.

While Roland hesitated, Jane jumped in. She was looking very white about the nose and mouth and her voice had gone up. 'I asked Roland for help. I decided that it would stir up more mud if I went to the police before I had all the available facts.'

Roland felt that it was his turn to help out. 'Ideally,' he said, 'what we would like to do is to prove that the sheriff was right and your . . . GG died by accident.' He paused before deciding to plunge ahead. 'But until we get much nearer to the truth we can only go on by eliminating people who were close to him. It would be very helpful if you could give us your accounts of that evening. Each of you may have seen or heard something that would help.' He glanced anxiously towards Jane but she was looking pleased and nodding at him.

The Ross Grants conferred by no more than a glance but evidently they were of a single mind. They set about finishing their sweet course. 'This seems to be a family matter,' Sheila said. 'We'll go and leave you to discuss it in privacy.'

'But you're family,' Jane said. 'You should be among the first to be concerned.'

Roland decided that he and Jane looked like becoming rather a good team. To his surprise, Violet jumped in on her sister's side. 'But you can't eat and leave like that,' Violet said in an innocent tone. 'That would be very rude. You haven't had your coffee yet and Manfred has been saving a special brandy for your visit.'

'We don't feel like prolonging our visit,' Ross said. Sheila added, 'You seem to be insinuating something.'

Violet looked very innocent. 'What could we possibly insinuate? Jane just wants to build up a picture of who saw or heard what on that evening.'

'Exactly,' Jane said. 'Surely you've nothing to hide?'

'Nothing at all,' Ross said. 'But we still have the right to resent any implication that we might have some knowledge . . .'

'Of the crime?' Violet said. 'Isn't that what you were going to say?'

'If you're going to put words into our mouths –' Ross began. Sheila finished the sentence for him. '– we're leaving,' she said flatly. The Grants rose in unison and made for the door.

Just before it closed, Roland said, 'Significant, do you think?'

With equal clarity Jane said, 'Oh, definitely.'

The door was jerked back again and Sheila's head re-appeared, followed by her body and, after a delay, her husband. 'What was that supposed to mean?' she asked shrilly.

'Listening, were you?' Violet remarked, although there could have been little doubt that the comment had been intended for the Grants to hear. 'You may as well come back in and have your coffee while we discuss it.'

Roland decided that, whatever differences there might have been, the two sisters could have made a formidable pair at poker. Ross and Sheila showed every sign of wishing to leave in a huff and yet quite determined that the discussion should not continue behind their backs. Manfred produced a decanter of what he described as a very good brandy although Roland, whose father had fancied himself a connoisseur, rated it somewhere in the cheaper half of the brandies, distilled from a definitely inferior wine. Manfred was revealing a talent for mime. His body language invited the pair to reseat themselves with such persuasiveness that they found themselves back in their chairs.

Instead of the argument that Roland had expected, there was a silence that he felt obliged to break. 'Surely,' he said, 'you can see that a flat refusal to discuss can only make things look worse. Of course, that's assuming that you're perfectly innocent. Only the guilty have a reason for silence.'

That line of argument, which might well have provoked an explosion, fell flat. Ross sneered. 'That's the same old argument that the police always produce – and the thriller writers. I could give you a string of reasons why somebody innocent of any particular offence might refuse to speak out. But we weren't trying to defend somebody else; or to protect ourselves against quite a different accusation. We simply do not take kindly to being suspected of any kind of wickedness on no grounds at all. Or do you have grounds? If so, let's have them out in the open. Is this something that you dreamed up while you were poking around with that Fiddler person?'

'We've no more reason to suspect you as against anyone else,' Jane said. 'We've never suggested that we had. But you had a relationship to GG – a rather distant relationship,' she amended quickly as Ross began to inflate. 'But you also move around among the people he knew and visited. Is it unreasonable of us to start by asking you what you can tell us about how he got on with those people, what quarrels there may have been and who might have had anything to gain – or might have thought that he had something to gain – by his death? Well?'

Ross sighed. 'No,' he said reluctantly. 'I suppose it's not unreasonable. I'm sorry if we went off half-cocked. But what reason do you have for believing that your great-granddad was killed?'

Violet emitted an unladylike grunt. 'That is what I was going to ask,' she said. Apparently the sibling truce was over.

Jane sat up straight. 'I don't just *believe* that he was murdered,' she said. Roland suddenly saw the danger that she was walking into. He tried to send her signals to shut up, by body language or telepathically, but they passed her by. 'I know that he was murdered,' Jane said. 'And I have evidence.'

'What evidence?' Violet demanded. She was supported by grunts of agreement from Ross and his wife.

Roland managed to attract Jane's attention and give her a ferocious frown. 'I can't possibly tell you that,' she said.

'Because there isn't any,' Sheila said.

Roland was in no doubt that Jane was about to burst forth and he was sure that it was too early for the details of their exploration with Ronnie to be made public. 'Don't let them provoke you,' he said firmly. 'Let's just make it clear that the evidence is locked away safely. I have one question. The last time that Jane saw GG, he started to say something. Can anybody tell me what it was?'

'No,' Violet said loudly. At the same moment Manfred said, 'It was about the house.' His wife was glaring at him. He subsided but surfaced again to mutter, 'Only about the money locked up in it.'

That was quite enough for battle lines to be drawn up. Soon it was Jane and Roland who made their escape, leaving the other two couples to vilify them as they liked. They found it interesting that none of what Mrs Cadwallader might have seen, deduced or guessed had been mentioned.

As soon as they were out in the sweet night air, Roland drew several deep breaths. There had been something about the atmosphere in that company that made him feel as if the oxygen was being sucked out of him. He had expected to know by instinct that somebody was lying but the only lie that he could detect had been about the brandy.

ELEVEN

Jane and Roland walked back to Birchgrove under a waning moon. At first they were silent, digesting the evening's events. Then Jane said, 'I blew it, didn't I?'

Roland balanced her self-esteem against possible dangers. Caution won. 'I'm afraid you did, a bit. I don't think that too much damage was done, because half the district seems to know that we're asking around, but most of them are too polite to ask us direct questions. Not later than the middle of tomorrow morning the news will be all over the neighbourhood that you claim to have evidence.' While he was speaking the implications were clarifying in his mind. 'Whoever killed your great-grandfather will know if he doesn't know now. From now on we shall have to watch our backs. But the question is, what will the guilty party think and do? He or she – let's assume *he* for the sake of simplicity – may not believe that we have anything. Or he may believe that you only have evidence that murder was done but not as to who did it – which is the case – and that if he sits tight nobody will think of him; but that's highly unlikely unless his motive is so remote that it's unlikely to surface. But he's just as likely to disbelieve, quite rightly, my statement that the evidence is tucked away safely – which is what we'd better do as soon as we get home. We have everything written down on computer and the digital photographs are safely in your camera, which is only safe for the moment. I suggest that we email the whole lot to the police and let it be known that we've done so.'

'I do have the email address of the local detective inspector,' Jane said.

'Home or business?'

'Both. GG knew him well. I know him too. Years ago I was lowered headfirst down a well to help rescue a boy who'd got himself into trouble and he was on the case.'

'That was you?'

'I was the only person small enough.'

Roland recalled what had been a cause célèbre at the time. He remembered thinking, *that's the sort of girl I should marry, when that time comes*. He had been very young. He pushed the thought aside. 'Email him a note to explain the photographs and then send them to him. I'll send you my summary of progress so far, for onward relaying.'

'That should do it.'

'It may not do it at all,' Roland said sternly. 'You're still not thinking. It must have been that cheap gin. You heard them guessing that whatever we found happened while Ronnie was helping us. Knowing his special talent, it wouldn't take too much of a leap to guess that he found whatever it was and that, if he wasn't available to speak to it, its value as evidence would be largely lost. If the villain sets out to cover his tracks, one of his first actions might be to dispose of Ronnie.'

'Kill him, you mean? You're right and I'm an idiot,' Jane said with unaccustomed humility. 'It must've been that gin. I'll phone him straight away and tell him to climb a tree and pull it up after him.'

Those words nearly started a train of thought that might have solved the case forthwith, but they were interrupted. The lights of a car, coming from the direction of Birchgrove, suddenly played around them, seeming impossibly bright in the darkness. Roland grabbed Jane's arm and jerked her towards the ditch. Knowing the road much better than he did, Jane leaned her weight back to slow him down, barged him to one side and brought them to a halt between two substantial sycamores with the ditch yawning at their feet. A car swept past and darkness returned.

'That was Miss Whetstone's car,' Jane said when she had recovered her breath. 'You could have recognized the rattles.'

Roland was still inclined to be suspicious. 'What would she be doing on this road at this time of night?'

The conversation was being conducted *sotto voce* but Jane lowered her voice still further. 'She's in a lesbian relationship with a woman who lives away at the bottom end of the valley, so whenever the husband goes out for the evening . . .'

'The Miss Whetstone who lives three doors from me?' Roland sounded shocked. 'But she must be about ninety.' To youth, even middle age seems to be astonishingly ancient.

'She is, or heading in that direction. Sixty, if she's a day. But what's that got to do with the price of fish?'

Lacking a cogent answer, Roland reverted to the original topic. 'We'd better see your detective inspector friend together,' he said, 'as soon as I've managed to summarize what we've got so far. After which, we'll probably be at loose ends again, except that Simon Parbitter's publisher wanted a chapter added to the book and I've got to copy-edit it. Would we be safe to walk the dogs again before bedtime?'

'Why not? Nobody's had time to come after us since the beans got spilled.' Roland tried to give her a look of reproof but they could hardly make each other's features out in the poor moonlight. 'It's perfectly clear that our secret was out from the moment that Mrs Cadwallader saw Ronnie in the tree. She must have discussed it with her neighbours, to judge by the speed with which our interest became known to everybody round about. But being interested is one thing, getting somewhere with it is quite another, so yes, I think Ronnie should be warned.'

Despite Roland's reasoning, they did take the dogs out again, their sole precautions being that Roland carried a heavy stick and Jane her rechargeable lantern. 'You phoned Ronnie?' Roland asked. The moon had set. He kept his voice down to a murmur in case ears were listening in the darkness or behind windows that were open in the stuffy air.

'I tried, but he's up north with a party of salmon anglers, which should be safe enough. Then I started up my computer, ready to send off those photographs, but there was an incoming message. Come round this way,' Jane muttered, taking his arm and shepherding him round a corner, 'and we'll keep the benefit of the street lighting, such as it is. The computer used to belong to my step-grandmother but it was better than mine so I kept it. My computer used a version of Windows that was replaced when GG was still in short trousers. I'm still sometimes getting her emails from people who hadn't heard about her death. This one was from an agent who sometimes used to let her house for her after she moved in with GG. Shooting parties in the winter and fishing in the summer. He's offering a jolly good rent for a fortnight's let to a quartet of salmon anglers.'

'Are you going to take it? Where will you go?' Roland had a sudden fear that she might be moving away. He wondered if he dared invite her to use his spare bedroom.

'I can't move out,' Jane said. 'I've made so many alterations to suit my veterinary work – tiling, secure cupboards for drugs and so on. But the money could be useful to us both. Your house is almost identical to mine. We could offer them that one. How would you like to occupy my spare bedroom? We'll split the rent, fifty-fifty.'

Roland could not find words to express how much he would like to sleep in Jane's spare bed, so he just said that it was a good idea. 'When does it start?'

'There's the rub. Their first booking let them down – an accidental double booking – so they're in a hurry. We'd have three days.'

If they had only had three hours, Roland would still have jumped at it. 'But I have quite a lot of stuff that will have to be put into store,' he said.

'I have a garage in the garage court. My car can stand out.'

'That sounds perfect. Let's get back and you can send an acceptance, offering an almost identical house with a slightly better outlook.'

He heard Jane chuckle. 'No hurry. The agent won't be in his office for another ten hours or so.' But she turned back anyway. 'We can prepare our emails for sending and start packing up. I can foresee a few busy days ahead.'

*   *   *

During the night, Jane slept deeply but Roland heard the sound of klaxons. Whether these were telling of the passing by of fire appliances, police cars or ambulances he could not be sure. That question was soon answered. He rose early in order to be ready for Mr Holmes, the gamekeeper, who would be coming to collect Sandy.

Mr Holmes arrived late and only added to the puzzles. 'I had a job and a half getting past Whinmount,' he said. 'Damn great fire engine and a police car blocking half the road.'

Roland felt his insides swoop down. Had he and Jane between them brought disaster onto her family? 'Was anybody hurt?' he asked.

The keeper shrugged. 'Not that I know of.'

'There was no ambulance standing by?'

'I didn't see one.'

In Roland's limited experience, an ambulance would have stood by to remove a body after the investigators had satisfied themselves. What was he going to tell Jane? 'Was the house much damaged?' he asked.

The keeper's eyebrows vanished under his woollen cap. 'The house? Not a damn bit. It was the tree, man. Yon big cedar that stood by the wee bridge.'

Roland blew out a huge breath of relief. 'A lightning strike?'

'Doubt it. The place was stinking of petrol. They wouldn't let me linger for a good look but it seemed to me that somebody had built a fire around the base, of brushwood and fallen sticks. Then he soaked the lot in petrol and dropped a match. Damned if I can think what anyone would want to do that for. The tree's still standing but it's its own shadow. I doubt it'll survive. The bark's too much damaged, and the bark of a tree is its circulation. See you this evening. Come, Sandy.'

Jane would not be waiting for him to join her for a dog walk. He phoned her number and got no reply so he hurried outside and managed to intercept her on the corner. The day was cooler, so she was wrapped in a warm parka. Roland deferred speaking until he could be sure that they were out of the general earshot, which proved to be a mistake. 'I phoned for Ian Fellowes,' she said quietly. 'The detective inspector, you know? But he's away at a conference in Glasgow for the whole week so we won't be able to have a session with him just yet and I don't want to say much to his staff until he says so because you can never be sure who's going to run to the media or, more importantly, who isn't, so I asked his wife – I get on very well with her, by the way – I asked her to get him to phone me the minute he gets back and I think we should email what we've got to his mobile number and there's a woman chief inspector in Edinburgh, the one they call Honeypot, and I think we could trust her—'

'Hoy!' said Roland. Jane broke off, breathing deeply, and blinked at him. 'You won't have heard the latest,' he said. 'Somebody torched your cedar tree during the night.'

Jane stopped so suddenly that King Coal bumped into the back of her knees. 'Clever!' she said. 'Without committing any more assaults or leaving any clues, he gets rid of all the physical evidence. Yes?'

'Not quite. We still have the photographs. I hope your camera's safe.' (Jane opened her parka and revealed her camera nestling between her neat breasts.) 'So far so good,' he said. 'And I hope that Ronnie's a good photographer.'

'He is,' Jane assured him. 'He worked with GG on two wildlife books and GG admitted that during the last few years his own hand was beginning to shake. He said that Ronnie had a grip as steady as a boulder. And cedar bark is soft so the marks of nylon line being pulled over it should be conspicuous.'

'He'd need his steady grip if he was trying to record the cuts made in bark by nylon monofilament, especially while balancing in the branches of a tree. Well, we'll just have to hope for the best. I think we'd better get back and email everything to your pal the detective inspector. I'm sorry about the tree, though. It did a lot for the view,' Roland was surprised to hear himself say. The countryside must be getting under his skin.

*   *   *

Jane had no facilities for printing her photographs. Violet
was the photographer in the family but Jane did not dare
to ask for her help. Now that she was away from Whinmount
it had been Jane's intention to take her camera to the local
chemist for the making of selected prints. The images as
seen on the camera's own viewfinder seemed very sharp.
They could only hope for the best and email them off to
DI Fellowes's mobile number and his home email address.
Jane also emailed them to Roland's computer and her own
in the hope of added safety. No murderer could hope to
intercept so many copies.

The next few days were marked by frantic activity. Roland
was being hounded by Simon Parbitter, who was being
hounded by his publisher while trying to complete his next
book against a deadline. Between bouts of copy-editing,
Roland contrived to separate the essentials for survival from
what would have to go into store to clear his house for the
fishing tenants. Jane went on the scrounge for cardboard
cartons, packed them and spent many hours transferring
cartons by car to the lockup garage or by hand to her own
house, finishing with an emergency clean and tidy of
Roland's house.

On the second afternoon she had made enough progress
for the moment. She took an hour off and drove down to
the Square. (Leaving the car outside the front door might
not be the best therapy for the rusty patches. It was also
too convenient. The habit of jumping into it for every little
journey was becoming too established. The needle on the
fuel gauge seemed determined to sink to zero.) She rather
hoped that Deborah Fellowes would have been left in charge
of the shop, and for once fate had been good to her. Deborah
glanced up, winked and went back to selling pigeon decoys
to a fat man with glasses.

When the deal was concluded and the client had gone
on his way, the two exchanged greetings. Deborah noticed
immediately that Jane was not dressed for visiting. 'Is this
a social call or can I sell you a fishing rod?' she asked. She
guided Jane in the direction of one of the pair of bentwood
chairs that awaited the bottoms of clients.

'Neither. I've no money and not a lot of time. I was rather hoping to find your father in charge here.' (This was a black lie. Jane was intimidated by Keith Calder and found his daughter more willing to give help without prising out the rest of the story.)

'Oho!' said Deborah. 'So it's about your late great-granddad. We hear over the grapevine that you're making enquiries. And about time too. Dad said when it happened that there was more to his death than met the eye.' Another finger on the mythical foot!

Jane reviewed and discarded the first dozen or so replies that came to mind. 'I would like a little help,' she said, 'but in total confidence. Except for your father,' she conceded. Her hope of enforcing silence between father and daughter was negligible. 'And your husband,' she added hastily. 'And please don't ask me to explain. It's a long shot, but I'd like to know if anyone who doesn't usually fish bought both eighteen pound and six pound monofilament recently.'

Deborah took on the look of a cat that is just about to swallow the canary. 'Is that how it was done? And then the big cedar catches fire during the night. I'll be damned. And you want to know who's been buying monofilament.' She exchanged knowing looks with a rubber owl decoy that squatted on a high shelf. 'It couldn't have been a simple tripwire because he wouldn't need two different sizes, so—'

'I'm not telling you any more until you tell me what I want to know.'

'That's all right. Ian will have it out of you in a jiffy.'

'He was going to get it from me the moment he got back anyway.'

'That's still all right,' Deborah said. 'He's at home now. I'll hear all about it tonight. He phoned a minute ago to find out if I knew where you are. Nobody else does. I don't remember anyone buying those sizes of monofilament but I'll ask Dad and Walter and have a look through the copy receipts.'

'Thanks,' Jane said. She fled the shop.

*   *   *

No more than a spoonful of precious petrol could have been wasted in Jane's detour past Roland's house, which showed no sign of an occupant. There was nobody awaiting her return at her house. She telephoned Ian Fellowes's house without receiving any other answer than from his machine. The telephonists at Police HQ were adamant that DI Fellowes was still in Inverness or possibly Aberdeen. Jane was in her hyped-up mood of riding roughshod over every stumbling block and she had no intention of sitting and waiting for Ian Fellowes to try again. She was considering which of the outstanding tasks she could most profitably tackle when her telephone demanded attention.

The caller was Mr Holmes, the keeper, wishing to know when Jane was going to deal with the dispatch and dismemberment of his sow. Well, so be it; perhaps it was a sign from Heaven. She replied that she was coming forthwith. The usual contrariness of fate should have brought everybody to her door at that juncture, but her luck held. She put a message on the DI's answering machine to the effect that she would be unavailable for several hours, left an envelope containing a similar message and addressed to the DI protruding from her own letter slot and pushed a note through Roland's door explaining her absence.

She found the keeper waiting, as promised, near his pigpen, complete with the implements that Jane had specified. The doomed porker was unwittingly enjoying a last meal while they discussed such matters as where and for how long the carcass was to hang. The keeper then left, rather hurriedly so as to be out of earshot when the deed was done. Jane pulled on the plastic overalls that usually protected her clothes during surgical operations.

The traditional method would have been to cut the pig's throat and let it bleed into a bucket, but Jane was not so hard-hearted. Fatima allowed herself to be led into a shed that was at least clean and smelling of disinfectant, where she was suddenly stunned by a blow from a heavy hammer.

It had taken Ian Fellowes less than a minute to extract her destination from Roland, who was not practised at resisting interrogation by the police. Jane did not know the keeper's pigs individually and she had assumed that one of the smaller porkers was to be disposed of; but the pig singled out by the keeper was definitely heavy. When Ian made his appearance, she had found herself quite unable unassisted to hang the pig from the beam – an operation that required her to lift the still unconscious pig one-handed while hauling the rope over a beam with the other hand. 'Thank God you're here!' she said. Ian's immediate impression that the cadaver was human and that she required his help in dealing with it was soon dispelled. 'Pull on this rope,' Jane resumed, 'while I lift.' She prepared to take the grisly object in her arms.

It seemed to be rather a hefty burden for a young lady. 'You'd better let me do the lifting,' Ian said.

'No. You don't want to get blood all over your nice suit.'

Ian thought that the citizens of Newton Lauder were some-times disappointed that their local detective inspector never showed any traces of his sometimes gruesome profession, but she did have a point. He hauled on the rope while Jane lifted. When poor Fatima was secured, hanging head down from the beam, Jane, while still bustling about, said, 'What are you doing here?'

'Did you think that you could email me statements like those and not have me hotfoot it back here?'

'Probably not. But for now, just go away. Sit in your car until I come and find you.'

Ian had an accurate notion of Jane's character. He had satisfied himself, years earlier, that she might be naughty, she might even put a toe over the strict boundaries of the law but she would never be wicked. He left the shed.

We need not concern ourselves too much with the gory details of what followed. Suffice it that a few minutes later Fatima had bled her last into a bucket and was now protected by a large muslin bag from any flies that made it past the outer defences of the shed. Jane drew off her latex gloves, struggled out of the overalls and washed at the sink. Outside, she found Ian relaxing in the driving seat of his Vectra and enjoying the sights and sounds of summer.

'Right,' he said through the open window. 'Now hop in and tell me about it.'

'I thought that our statements and photographs said it all. Did the photographs turn out all right?'

'Razor sharp. Whoever took them is a skilled photographer.'

'Ronnie Fiddler took them. Well, I'm at a loose end until the corpse cools enough for me to start cutting it up. Let's get back to my house so that I can get a proper wash.'

'There was a sink in a corner of the shed.'

'Cold running water and God alone knows where the water comes from,' said Jane. 'I don't wish to infect all the local citizens with typhoid. Some of them, but not all. Follow me home.'

The DI followed. He rather agreed with her sentiment regarding the local population.

TWELVE

Jane was relieved to see her own front door standing ajar, indicating the return of Roland. She led Ian Fellowes inside and gave the DI a seat in the sitting room where already Roland's computer was established on the window table, its screen alight but dourly blank. It seemed a very long time since she remembered eating. Ian Fellowes admitted that he had been home for a meal. Roland, who she met at the bottom of the stairs, confessed to hunger but stoutly insisted that, apart from a few cartons in his hall awaiting removal to Jane's garage, his house was ready for the visitors and that all that he would need during the next few weeks was stored in the spare room upstairs.

'Why did you have to tell that busybody policeman where I was?' she whispered. Aloud she asked, 'So we're all ready for the visitors?'

'Yes.' He dropped his voice. 'Why did it matter?'

She dropped hers even lower. 'Because I was breaking the law. So you sleep here tonight?' she asked loudly. She sent him into the sitting room to keep the DI out of mischief while she made a plate of sandwiches, using supermarket bread and pâté (both slightly outdated), lettuce from her own garden with tomatoes from the garden of a neighbour who had rashly gone on holiday leaving his greenhouse unlocked. When she brought a heavy tray into the sitting room with the sandwiches, her largest teapot and three mugs, the low table in front of Ian Fellowes was already covered with photographs and printed pages. Jane gave Roland the tray to hold while she brought out a nesting table.

The DI accepted tea and absent-mindedly helped himself to a sandwich. 'Let's see if I've got this straight. Not knowing whether or not you had usable photographs of the marks in the bark of the tree, you announced that you possessed evidence that your great-grandfather had been murdered.

Almost immediately the tree, aided by a dousing with petrol, went up in flames.'

'That seems to be true so far,' Jane said.

The DI drew himself up without going to the length of standing. Evidently reproof was about to be delivered from on high, backed by the majesty of the law. 'This is not the first time that you and your family have decided to conduct your own investigations, bypassing the proper authorities. And now look what's come of it.'

Jane was not going to let him get away with that. 'What has come out of it is a burned tree, after it had been carefully photographed, plus the conclusions that you can draw from that event. You're always complaining that you're understaffed. You're well known for inducing members of the public to investigate each other for you. I've heard you laughing about it yourself.'

'What's more,' Roland said, 'you must have pronounced yourselves satisfied that it was an accident before the sheriff would have brought in that verdict. If she – we – hadn't begun to ask questions a murder would have been overlooked. You haven't lost any evidence so far as we know, but the fact that the tree was set on fire confirms Jane's story and gives you a starting point that you didn't have before.'

'I don't see what you're getting at,' the DI said stiffly, avoiding eye contact with either of them.

'I think you do. You're not dim, in fact I have heard you described, not looking at anybody in particular, as a clever but devious bastard. All that you had before would have been a theory, some faint marks, several weeks old, in the trunk of a tree and possibly a record of somebody buying nylon monofilament. Nothing to offer Forensics at all. Now you've got fresh evidence of somebody setting a fire.'

Ian Fellowes curled his lip. 'And I'm supposed to go round these worthy citizens, sniffing for petrol traces and looking for soot?'

Roland was ready with an angry reply but Jane anticipated him. 'Leave it, Roland,' she said. 'I've seen this modus operandi before. He wants to make us feel guilty so that we'll do his work for him.'

'I don't have to make you feel guilty,' said the DI. 'I need only have mentioned the meat inspector. But I preferred to do it the nice way.'

'You needn't have done it at all. The more convinced I become that my darling GG was killed, the angrier I get. He wasn't just my great-grandfather. He was my father and mother. He was my guide, philosopher and friend.' Her voice broke.

Instead of following his instinct and hugging her to him, Roland took over the argument. 'You don't have to dash around looking for contact traces. You could start with Mrs Young, her husband and the other couple who were at her dinner and find out who they told about Jane's statement that she had evidence, and then find out who Mrs Cadwallader had told about seeing Ronnie Fiddler up in the tree.'

'That,' said Ian Fellowes, 'is just the kind of task that I'll be happy to delegate to the two of you. And then you can ask each of them who they told, and so ad infinitum. If there's anybody within ten miles who doesn't figure on at least one list, I'll be amazed.'

Roland seemed to hear an echo of Jane's voice saying *the fingers of one foot*. 'You may be absolutely right,' he said. 'But if it comes to asking a thousand people ten thousand questions, that's your job rather than ours.'

'These are my friends and neighbours,' Jane pointed out. 'If I start asking that sort of question, even over the teacups, I'll get some short, sharp answers.'

The DI considered mentioning the meat inspector again, but the presence of a witness turned the uttering of even implicit threats into a danger area. 'I simply do not have staff for that sort of enquiry,' he said weakly.

Jane knew where to find his Achilles heel. 'Then you'll just have to take the one step that you hate and ask Edinburgh for help,' she said.

Ian Fellowes tried not to show a disgusted face. Jane was quite right. From the moment that the enquiry changed from a precautionary re-examination of the facts surrounding an accidental death and into an investigation of a possible

murder, Edinburgh would take over. A hostile and probably
critical superintendent would bring in his own team. The
local Crime Section, all four of them including Ian, would
be relegated to a support role, fetching and carrying, seeking
the answers to almost certainly irrelevant questions and
providing local knowledge. They would be forced to stand
back and watch while carefully nurtured relationships with
local citizens and informants were blown to the winds. He
had seen it all before and he was not going to face it again
until he had so much evidence that Edinburgh would treat
the solution as a fait accompli. Otherwise, any media
releases would be carefully constructed and manned by
chosen personnel. Credit for a successful conclusion would
be retained in Edinburgh but the blame for an unsolved
crime would rest with the officer who had raised the alarm
in the first place.

He gathered up his dignity. 'That approach would almost
certainly turn out to be taking a sledgehammer to crack a
nut.'

'The police are well known for taking sledgehammers to
nuts,' Jane said.

'Usually the nuts of reluctant witnesses,' put in Roland.
'We wouldn't dream of infringing on your copyright.'

'That doesn't mean that we're unwilling to help,' Jane
said. 'As your better half has probably told you, we've
already started an enquiry going as to who bought two
different weights of nylon monofilament line. Of course,
that may have come off the reels in the bottom of somebody's fishing bag, in which case I may be better placed
than you are to know who goes in for that sort of fishing.'

Ian, who had his own sources of such information
including his father-in-law, merely nodded. 'And what other
contribution are you preparing to make?'

Jane found that that part of her mind had gone blank,
taken over by a fresh anger that her beloved GG had been
done to death. She looked enquiringly at Roland, who rushed
to her rescue again. 'Whoever set this trap,' he said, 'would
have had to climb that tree earlier in daylight, to set it up.
Our contact with the local gossips is certainly better than

yours but I wouldn't count on turning up any witnesses –
it need not have taken him long and parts of the tree are
thick enough that if he was dressed in drab colours and
kept still it would be very unlikely that any passer-by would
notice him. Then he would have had to lurk, unless he was
so callous that he didn't care who got killed. He couldn't
just go home to bed, there would be a strong possibility
that somebody else would walk into the trap. In daylight
he'd hide in the hollow between the boulders. If the proverbial innocent bystander came along he could slack off the
trigger string. Jane, what would you say was the probability of GG being the first person to cross the bridge?'

Jane forced herself to concentrate. 'GG was the most
regular walker by that route, especially late in the evening.
If you made me guess, I'd say six or seven chances out of
ten. Maybe eight.'

Roland nodded emphatically. 'There you are. GG was
late going for his walk that evening. So who was absent
from home during a period of several hours? Who was
dawdling within sight of the bridge, either hidden or looking
very innocent? Which leads on to another very interesting
question. Was GG really the intended victim or did he walk
into a trap intended for somebody else? And consider this.
A body blow followed by a fall into cold water among
rocks would certainly prove fatal to a very old man. To an
athletic younger man, say a rugby player, even serious injury
would be much less likely. Does some other very old man
walk that path at night?

'Then there's the question of motive. We have seen hardly
a trace of a motive. He would seem to have been one of
those rare individuals of whom their obituaries say that they
were beloved by everybody. In his case, it sounds as though
it might even have been true. But unless the whole thing
was an accident wrapped in coincidences or a practical joke
that went tragically wrong, there is somebody walking
around who had, or thought he had, a good reason to want
Mr Grant . . . out of the way. The will may reveal more of
a motive for somebody. Could you not get a sight of it?'

Fellowes looked as though he had trodden in a dog-turd.

'I've tried, believe it or not, but lawyers have their own ways of stalling the release of information.'

'It is entirely up to Jane,' Roland said, 'because this is a matter concerning her family, but my own feeling is that, if she wishes, we would have more chance of picking up information about peoples' motives and movements in the course of friendly gossip than you would have in formal interviews.'

Ian Fellowes had been watching Roland's face. He switched his eyes to Jane. 'Well?'

Jane produced a shuddering sigh. 'I started asking questions because I couldn't bear the idea of my great-grandfather's death being written off as an accident while his murderer sits at home, gloating. I wanted somebody to do something. That, Inspector, means you. I asked Roland to help me because I had no idea how to go about it. I don't think he realizes it, but Roland has been a huge help already, introducing method into my rather shambolic thinking. I think he's able to think freely just because he doesn't have any personal involvement. If he's willing to go on helping, I don't mind doing just as he suggested and talking to people –' there was a pause while she took a deep breath, '– but we still have to survive and he has to be free to get on with his writing and I have to take on any veterinary jobs when Mr Hicks isn't available. It's all getting rather difficult and perhaps you'd better let Edinburgh take over after all.'

Fellowes' frown became a furious scowl. 'I can't expect you to investigate and come up with a complete case. That would be my job. If you can bring me a name along with at least some reasons to believe in that person's guilt, it will be up to me to do the rest.' The DI's gaze flicked back to Roland. 'Miss Highsmith hasn't given you much chance to say whether you're willing to help her or not.'

When Jane paid her tribute to the value of Roland's help, she had shot him a glance that pierced him through, embodying gratitude and, he dared to hope, admiration. He longed to say that there was nothing he wanted more than to help; that he would be bitterly hurt if she looked to anyone else for any kind of support; that for another such glance he would uproot what remained of the cedar tree and use it to belabour anyone who gave her the least offence. But the words stuck in his throat. He could have embodied them in a novel or in the libretto for an opera; but they were, he now realized, too close to his heart to be said aloud. He began to mutter a speech suggesting that Jane could always count on him, got lost in a confusion of syntax and let his voice trail away. His hearers seemed to understand.

THIRTEEN

Roland saw the detective inspector to the door and returned, frowning over a page of paper apparently torn out of a school exercise book.

Jane was back at the sink, drying dishes. 'Where do you think we go from here?' she asked over her shoulder.

Roland looked at his watch. 'Our visitors should be here by now. We'd better make sure that they're not too unhappy. After that, you may feel that this needs following up. It was on the mat. It's from Bart Hepworth.'

'My dog fight client? Read it out to me.'

'It's rather rambling, verbose and misspelled and his hand-writing would probably be more legible to someone who's as drunk as he seems to have been when he wrote it. After puzzling it out once, I don't feel like making the effort again. The gist is that a young boy and girl usually meet on top of the mound beyond the bridge most evenings and he believes that they saw something. "After school," he says.'

It was Jane's turn to consult her watch. It took her only a few seconds to sort out her priorities. 'We have time in hand. You dash round to your house make sure that the tenants have arrived and are happy, or if they're not happy at least make sure that they sign the inventory that I left in the top left-hand drawer in your kitchen and that they aren't unhappy enough to make a fuss. Meanwhile I'll be sorting out my fishing gear.'

'Why—?'

'It's time that you had that casting lesson. Then we can have a snack. And after that, there may be an evening rise beginning. Insects often hatch in the evening so that they'll have the hours of darkness when predators can't grab them . . . All right,' Jane said irritably. 'You don't have to look at me as though I've gone bonkers. I have my reasons, you could have trusted me.'

Roland began to wonder whether this girl was worthy of his devotion. 'I do trust you,' he said. 'I would trust you with my life. But can I trust you to come to the point?'

'I would have come to the point ages ago if you hadn't introduced the digression,' Jane said with dignity. 'If a young couple – and at least one of them must be very young if they meet after school, unless it's one of the teachers – if they meet after school they have reason to be secretive. They won't hang around if we're obviously watching for them. If we want to be inconspicuous, we can fish. There are trout there. Not many and not usually very big, but enough to justify a visit and introduce you to another source of free protein.'

'Don't we have to pay for fishing?' Roland asked cautiously.

'Not everywhere. There are places that don't belong to anybody, or if they do nobody knows it. In point of fact, Mr Holmes claims the fishing rights to the burn that runs past Whinmount and nobody's ever argued with him, but if he wants me to go on looking after that dog of his he'd better nod and smile.'

Dram was making progress but still sorry for himself. Jane checked the alignment of his vertebrae and worked his joints for a minute or two before telling the keeper that she and Roland would be fishing the burn. Mr Homes just nodded and almost smiled.

Jane's car had been left in a field gate near where Dram had met with his accident. Jane resumed the wheel and they crossed one field to where a line of silver birches showed where the burn ran. They began to prepare. Jane had her own waders but neither Violet nor her husband was interested in angling so Jane had kept those of her great-grandfather. They were nearly new and a passable fit for Roland. Jane's two rods, each originally the property of GG, were ready set up and carried on magnetic holders on the roof of Jane's car. It was a warm and humid evening, perfect, Jane said, for angling.

Roland soon mastered the trick of wading but he boggled

at the length of wading confronting him. 'Could we not have parked nearer to Whinmount?' he asked.

'Fish face upstream,' Jane said shortly. 'You want to sneak up on them. So we wade upstream.'

'Catching fish would be a welcome bonus but it's not really what we came out for.'

Jane sighed. She was still amazed to find how ignorant he could be about things that she seemed always to have known – things shown her by . . . She broke off the thought. This was no time for tears. 'Around here,' she said, 'the kids, boys especially, are born knowing about these things. Let's not sow doubts in their tiny minds.'

On the lawn Roland had soon picked up the basics of casting, even managing the timing required for the brook rod, so Jane sent him ahead with the short rod, following behind with the longer trout rod. The banks supported many trees and much undergrowth of gorse and weeds. Jane was twice caught up and Roland, even with the advantage of the shorter rod, seemed to spend much of the time disentangling his line from the gorse, with the result that Jane overtook him as they arrived below the pool where the burn emerged from the cleft, downstream of the burned cedar tree.

She decided to call a halt. They seated themselves on the bank with their feet in the water. 'If we go on losing flies at this rate,' Jane said, 'your next lesson will have to be fly-tying. Now, let's consider tactics. There may be no problem, but we don't want them to bolt as soon as they realize that they've been rumbled. I spent most of my childhood here, remember, so I know every inch. You work your way forward until you're a little short of the bridge. Opposite the bridge and about a couple of hundred metres away there's a sort of knoll which is hollow on top. It makes a nice sheltered spot to meet a boyfriend.'

Roland felt a pang of jealousy. 'Did you—?'

Jane laughed. 'Heavens, no! I was too young to have boyfriends and, anyway, as fast as I started to make friends Violet pinched them off me. You can see the approach to the knoll from this side of the bridge, or else you could pretend to be looking at the tree. Either way, when or if you see two figures climbing the knoll, give me a wave. I'll work round behind them.'

Roland thought it over and then agreed.

They had almost reached the hump that the road climbed over. The stream followed a natural fault in the bedrock and Roland was soon wading up a cleft that twisted between rocky walls. The stream was narrow and ran fast. It was clear of weed – and of fish. He forced his way against the faster current and came out in the more level ground and the broader and slower stream where they had sought out the evidence of GG's murder. The black skeleton of the tree reared up far ahead and the bridge began to show.

Roland had been casting with care, concentrating above all else on not getting his line caught up again in branches above or weeds below. He made a mistake. His line fell across a patch of waterweed with his fly bobbing just beyond. He had to move quickly or his fly would be into the weed. He lifted the rod and at that moment there was a plop! A fish had been waiting in the still water upstream of the weed for insects to be brought to it. The fly vanished into a pink mouth.

He tried to play the fish as Jane had explained to him but circumstances were against him. The stream was too narrow between rafts of weed. Roland, who could ill spare the time to learn another skill, was concentrating on not losing another fly. The zigzagging fish seemed to have pulling power far above its weight. The small rod bent into a hoop but the fish knew the water better than he did and had soon dug itself into the weed.

One thing was sure – the fish was not going anywhere for the moment. Roland only had to take one pace to the side and he could lay the rod on the bank. He rolled up his sleeves and felt his way along the fine nylon towards the hook. He came on the fish suddenly. The fish was as startled as he was and tried to leap. He nearly apologized. Roland knew that he should grip the fish by the gills but that somehow seemed too personal and possibly cruel and yet he was gripped by the anticipation of the hunter who already sees on his plate the meat that he hunted for himself. The fish was his to keep. The hook seemed to be firmly in place. He took a grip on the shank of the hook and with the other hand he began to free the nylon from the weed. Where possible, he tore the weed and let it float away.

He was jerked out of his concentration when a pair of waders appeared beside him and Jane was stooping over his catch with a word of approval. From one of the many pockets of her fishing waistcoat she produced a tool that was part scissors and part pliers. She grasped the fish just as Roland had hesitated to do, snipped the nylon close to the fly and then, holding the slippery fish over the bank in case it managed to thrash its way free, she produced a 'priest' from another pocket and gave it a sharp rap over the head.

'Nice one,' she said softly. 'Brown trout. About a pound, which is big for here. That takes care of our meal tonight.' She twisted the hook out of the fish's jaw and dropped the fish into her bag. The hook went into a pad of lambswool on her lapel. 'I think I saw the top of a head up there while you were preoccupied. I think they're there. I'm going to pretend to give up in disgust and head for the town. Like I said, I'll try to get behind them. You go on pretending to fish but head them off it they come this way.'

'Got you.'

Roland resumed casting but without the fly on the line. It came easier without the threat of being caught up in foliage, but probably looked less convincing. Facing upstream in accordance with Jane's edict, he was also facing the bridge. Jane had already reeled in. She poked the butt of her rod into the mud at the bottom of the stream and let the upper segments rest among the branches of an alder that overhung the water. She turned towards the bank and stepped into an unsuspected hole in the bed of the stream. Before she could save herself, she went down on her knees. Her thigh waders filled with water.

At least, she thought, it gave her an excuse to take to the footpath. 'I'll go home, change and come back,' she called to Roland. Walking in waders full of water is difficult and noisy. On the bank, she struggled out of the waders, emptied them and, leaving the waders and her socks, set off walking barefoot up the rough and narrow path that continued from the bridge and eventually, she knew, arrived by a devious route in Newton Lauder. A hundred paces from the bridge another and even less significant path led off towards the knoll and she turned onto it.

Jane had no very high opinion of the young. She had been young herself once and considered herself expert. She was quite prepared for a scene of depravity. Smoking probably. Sex certainly. As she approached, a girl's voice speaking softly became audible out of the evening silence. She was quoting Keats. *'The voice I hear this passing night was heard / In ancient days by emperor and clown.* What Jane saw came as a surprise. The girl was sprawled on the dry grass, her skirt tucked demurely around her knees and in her hand a paperback volume of poetry. Her straight hair had suffered a pudding-basin cut that made no concessions to the promised attractiveness of her features. The boy was kneeling, peering through the bracken to where Roland was patiently flogging the water.

'Good afternoon,' Jane said.

There was no guilty leaping apart. The girl looked up and smiled. Without turning his head the boy said, 'That was a good fish your friend landed, miss.' The pair, Jane thought, were in their mid-teens.

'Wasn't it just! And he's an absolute beginner. Life isn't fair!' In the space of half a second Jane revised her planned approach. A softer opening was called for. 'I'm hoping that you can give me some help. I'm told that you're quite often up here at about this time.'

The boy turned to face her and scowled. 'What about it? We're not doing anything wrong.'

'I can see that. So why be so secretive about it?'

'Can you see what sort of time my friends would give me if they knew that I was reading poetry with a girl?'

He had a point. Jane remembered her own schooldays at the same school. 'Yes, I can see that,' she said. 'But you can come and read poetry to me any time. Were you here on the evening before Mr Grant died? You know which evening that was?'

The boy turned and slid down into a sitting position. 'Of course we do. People were talking about it. Yes, we were here.'

'Please tell me what you saw or heard.'

'I didn't see anything,' the boy said disgustedly. 'It was my turn to read. John Donne. *Go and catch a falling star / get with child a mandrake root. / Tell me where all past years are / or who cleft the devil's foot,*' he quoted with relish.

Perhaps they were not so innocent after all, if they absorbed John Donne and could read him aloud with feeling.

'I didn't see a lot,' said the girl. 'Nothing of great interest. I was listening to Hugh. He reads beautifully. But I did see a man climb into the tree. The one that burned. Is that any good?'

'Was it someone you recognized?' Jane asked. The girl shook her head. 'What did he look like?'

'Nothing very much in particular. He was broad. Not fat but thickset. And he had a hat on and corduroys and a checked shirt.'

It wasn't much but it was a start. 'Did he climb easily? Or was it a great effort, as if he was old or sedentary?'

'Easily, as if he was athletic. Then he seemed to be messing about for ages but I couldn't make out what he was doing, it didn't seem to make any sense. He climbed up and down several times. When a lady with a poodle came past he sort of froze and she never noticed him. Then he tucked himself away in the hole between those boulders. But he smoked while he waited there. I could see the smoke drifting out. It was a bad evening for midges and he probably smoked to keep them away. He smoked two or three cigarettes while he was up in the tree – he just dropped them in the water and let the current carry them away. And he smoked about six more while he was among the rocks.'

Jane accepted the news with satisfaction. Cigarettes might mean DNA. 'Was there anything else that caught your attention? Did his ears stick out, for instance? Was his nose big or small?'

'Far as I can remember, his ears were flat to his head and his nose was small. That was all.'

Any further questions that Jane could think of, the girl answered quite openly but without taking her any further. At last, 'Thank you,' Jane said. 'You've been very helpful. If you remember anything else, put a note through my door. If it leads anywhere, there may be a reward.'

But don't hold your breath, she thought. The boy evidently picked up her thought. 'If there really would be a reward, you'd have asked her where she lives.'

'I know Jessie Donald,' Jane said, 'and this just has to be her daughter. She's the image of her mum. You must be Sheila. How's your kitten?'

'All right now, thank you. She's getting big.'

'I'd be worried if she wasn't. Is your mum still a district nurse?'

'No,' the girl said. 'There was too much travelling and too little nursing. She works at the cottage hospital now.'

FOURTEEN

Jane visited the hole between the boulders. She skinned her knee slightly. For a moment she was eight again. As Sheila Donald had said, there was a scattering of cigarette ends. Several of them were beneath an overhang of rock topped with bracken. The place was dry. Grass and wild flowers were flattened just where a dog would choose to lie and, going down on her knees, she saw what she took to be dog-hairs on a stem of bramble.

There was no longer a need for stealth. Jane was whistling as she returned to Roland. Her voice sounded cheerful as she relayed the description of the man in the tree. At last there was a light at the end of the tunnel. Even that poor description should be enough to identify the killer, or at least to eliminate many of the potential suspects. DNA on the cigarette ends might do the rest.

Roland had still been casting his hookless line over the water. 'We can pack up now,' Jane said. 'We've got what we came for – including your fish.' Roland grinned. Jane thought that she had presided at the birth of a committed angler.

To reach her rod, Jane had to recross the bridge and re-enter the water. The glutinous mud between her toes was another reminder of her childhood. She disentangled her line from the twigs with a silent curse on whatever gods decreed that nylon or polycarbonate line would always wrap itself around any object within reach. When she stepped back to the bank she felt a sting on the sole of her foot, which puzzled her. Jellyfish do not haunt fresh water. She crawled onto the bank, laid her rod down and looked over her shoulder.

'Roland,' she called. 'Come quickly.'

Roland was at her side almost immediately. He found her seated on the bank and using the scissors tool combination in attempting to cut off her left shirtsleeve. Infected by her obvious haste, he finished the job for her before looking down. Then he drew in a sharp breath. The gash in the sole of her left foot extended along the arch from the heel to the ball and as far as the toes. He could see bone. Under her direction he used the detached sleeve to bind the foot.

'Ambulance,' he said. 'You have your mobile?'

Jane extracted her mobile phone from among the many pockets of her fishing waistcoat. She keyed for the emergency services and in a voice that was calm but becoming hoarse she summoned an ambulance and described the place. 'Now help me up,' she told Roland.

'You can't possibly walk on that.'

'I can hop if you help me.'

Roland got his hands under her armpits. She was almost on her feet when she rolled her eyes back and became limp. Lacking a proper grip, he could only lower her onto her back. Blood was dripping from her foot again. He tightened the binding as much as he could and then contrived a tourniquet by cutting a length of line from his rod and inserting the 'priest' to tighten it. The dribble of blood diminished.

There was as yet neither sight nor sound of the ambulance. Time might prove precious. It might have been a good moment for the boy and girl to appear but it seemed that they had made their departure.

The ambulance did not have far to come but Jane was losing blood in a steady dribble. He tightened the binding around her foot again. Time was still obviously of the essence and she had set him an example of staying calm in a crisis. They were on the wrong side of the bridge. He pictured two ambulance men manoeuvring a stretcher over the narrow bridge and dropping it in the water along with its precious burden.

Cinema and TV heroes are often to be seen lifting unconscious girls in their arms but this is not as easy as it is made to look. Roland knelt beside her, put his arms under her knees and shoulders and lifted. So far was indeed so good, but when he tried to get on to his feet he found it impossible.

He set her down gently, rose to his feet, stooped and tried again. This time he was too successful and he landed on his back with the girl sprawled on top of him. He tried not to imagine the picture they would present if people in general and ambulance personnel in particular should arrive. He struggled free and retightened the pressure bandage.

For his next attempt he stood uptight with his hands under her armpits and lifted her. If she had been less limp the next move would have been easy, but the best that he could manage was a quick twirl that would have been better suited to the dance floor. He allowed her to fall forward over his shoulder into a fireman's lift. This was hardly the romantic attitude that his subconscious mind had been cherishing but at least it nearly worked.

He had already begun the crossing of the bridge, a crossing made more difficult by the descending sun shining into his eyes, when Jane, notwithstanding her loss of blood, grunted, stirred and began to struggle. To prevent her from sliding off his shoulder and following her great-grandfather into the water the best grip offered to him was around her bottom. His hands followed as she slid down his front. Her eyes were open and only inches away from his. 'Oh,' she said, 'it's you.' Roland tried to believe that her tone was of relief but the question was academic. She fainted again. This time, all that he could do was to clasp her firmly around the middle and struggle across the remainder of the bridge with her trailing legs trying to trip him and pitch the pair of them into the water.

He had just made it safely back to terra firma when the ambulance arrived. Its staff looked at him as though they were rescuing her from an abuser but he was past caring. He was relieved of his burden and of the available information. For the few yards remaining a stretcher was called into use. The ambulance reversed as far as the driveway of Whinmount, made its turn and pulled away. Jane would be taken to the local cottage hospital, at least in the first instance, but Roland had been given to understand that he need not bother telephoning for a progress report for several hours.

As the gaudy vehicle dwindled in the direction of the B-road, it came to Roland suddenly that he had a thousand things to do. One of his lecturers had been at pains to point out that even in literature the establishing of priorities was a necessity and had gone to some lengths in explaining the concept of the critical path network. Any sloppiness in plotting the time-line, he had said, would result in a return of disbelief to the reader. This had seemed to Roland to be so supremely logical that it had stuck in his mind and he now began to sort the outstanding tasks into sequence by creating a network in his head. It was still the gestation phase when the first and most urgent moves became obvious.

Hurrying clumsily in GG's waders he jogged along the road and over the hump. As, panting and sweating, he reached the gate to the field where Jane's Terios had been left, the keeper's Land Rover met him and Mr Holmes wound down his window. Sandy's big head appeared beside the keeper's and he barked once in recognition. 'You seem to be in a hurry,' remarked the keeper.

The pieces of Roland's half-formed programme fell apart and began to reassemble themselves. He began a hasty explanation of what had befallen Jane.

The keeper showed a hitherto unsuspected side of himself, both methodical and helpful. 'Let's take it a step at a time,' he said. 'You'll need transport but Miss Highsmith's car isn't insured for you. Hop in. I'll lift you to where she left her car. Then you drive this one – it's insured for any driver – and I'll drive hers to her house. My business in the town will take me an hour or maybe two. Then I'll come back for you and you drive this vehicle to the hospital and I'll follow you again in her little one and leave you there with her car. You go and see her and take in with you the phone number of her insurance company.'

'How—?'

Mr Holmes's demeanour showed a touch of impatience. 'It'll be on the tax disc holder. Have her phone them and get them to add you to her policy as an authorized driver, or whatever the term is. And the next little problem?'

'I don't know,' Roland admitted. 'Once I've got transport I should be able to solve most of them for myself.'

While they spoke, Roland had taken the passenger seat
and received a violent welcome from Sandy. Mr Holmes,
who was accustomed to off-road driving, had swung through
the gateway and set off across the bumps and hollows of
the field at such a pace that Roland was only saved from
hitting his head on the metal roof by Sandy, who as a form
of greeting, had forced his way between the seats and
sprawled across his lap.

They reached the Terios. Roland transferred to the driving
seat of the Land Rover and received a few basic instructions on how to drive a four-by-four and a warning about
the slippery quality of grass. They set off in convoy.
Mr Holmes was more considerate to Jane's car than he had
been to his own. At the bridge, the keeper waited while
Roland recovered rods and waders and other items of gear
and clothing. Ten minutes later these made an impressive
little pile by Jane's gate. The keeper even waited and helped
to carry them indoors.

'You'll have your hands full,' Mr Holmes said. 'I could
keep both dogs for you until she's back on both feet.'

'That would be very good of you.'

Holmes waved thanks away. 'Not in the least. She saved
my dog. If she wanted my left leg she could have it.'

'He's doing well, is he?'

'Better than I dared hope. See you in an hour or two.'

'Wait,' Roland said. 'Wait.' A passing neighbour was
looking at him with more than idle curiosity but Roland
was past caring. 'Listen.' As nearly as he could remember
it he repeated Jane's version of Sheila Donald's description
of the man in the tree. 'Does that ring any bells? Have you
seen him around Wedell, for instance?'

While he considered, the keeper stroked his chin,
producing a sound like somebody walking through dry
leaves. 'Not much of a description,' he said at last. 'Some
of it's of clothes, which change from day to day if you're
not going to smell him coming. I don't think that it could
be either of Ross Grant's sons but, the hours I work, I've

hardly set eyes on either of them. I'll think about it and keep my eyes open and I'll let you know.'

Roland carried the fishing gear indoors and put it away much as he thought Jane had produced it. When he came to removing the borrowed waders he discovered the reason for the passing neighbour's interest. Even Sandy's greeting had seemed muted. From collar to waders Roland was liberally spattered with Jane's blood. How the blood had come to encroach on his face and hair he never discovered, but in his mental network he moved a shower and change from low down on the list to the very top.

He returned downstairs thirty minutes later, much refreshed, with his ideas clarified and both beds made. He had eaten nothing since his breakfast. How to gut and fillet a trout was still a mystery to him so he put his trout in the freezer and got out some meat. He made a quick fry-up and, while he ate, he used the telephone. He notified the vet that Jane's services might not be available for an unspecified period and worked through her personal address book for anyone else requiring immediate notification. No doubt Jane and the mail between them would keep him primed.

Another phone call to the hospital, during which he blandly claimed to be Jane's partner, determined that Jane was receiving emergency treatment. She would be removed to Edinburgh later that afternoon for the necessary micro-surgery, but could be visited in an hour's time.

Whether Jane was to return home next day or in a month's time, he was determined that she would find the house clean and tidy. There was to be no room for cracks about a male slum. He fed Sandy and then filled the time with house-work until Mr Holmes returned.

The Newton Lauder Cottage Hospital is on a rural site, only a mile up the hill from Birchgrove. Roland pulled up at the main entrance while Mr Holmes parked in a remote corner and walked back to deliver the key of the Terios and accept in exchange some fervent thanks. Sandy returned to the Land Rover and Roland was careful to advise that no matter how emphatically Sandy insisted that he had not been fed, he was not a truthful dog and should be disbelieved.

Jane was discovered alone in a two-bed High Dependency room, dressed in a skimpy hospital gown. Blood was being dripped into her arm but she was otherwise free of attachments. Roland promised to call for help if there was any change and the nurse slipped away to enjoy an overdue cuppa and a forbidden cigarette.

Roland had the impression that Jane was still dopey from the anaesthetic. She blinked several times before recognizing him. Then she smiled. 'Thanks for coming, Roland,' she said. 'I seem to have trodden on a broken bottle and it took them longer to pick all the bits and grains of grit out than to repair the damage. I have the same problem with dogs. Actually, they haven't finished the patching up. Even with my vet's training I didn't realize how many nerves and sinews and arteries and veins and things the human foot has. The doctor who did the first part of the job came in to see me. I'm told that he's pretty hot stuff but he said that he was hard put to it to work out what should be joined to which. He said that if I found myself walking backwards I'd know that he'd got it wrong. I hope he was joking. God! I'm bloody well exhausted. And I'm colder than I've ever been. Must be loss of blood.'

'Your tongue seems to have recovered.'

'Am I talking too much again? It must be the stuff they give you to wake you up. It has quite an effect on . . .' She closed her eyes and fell asleep.

The fact that her bosom was rising and falling in a rhythmic and mildly erotic manner reassured Roland that she was still alive, but he was wondering whether he should call somebody when she said '. . . horses,' quite clearly.

Her eyes seemed to be focussed on him. 'Are you taking in what I'm saying?' he asked.

'I think so.' She blinked a dozen times in succession. 'You're Roland, right?'

'Got it in one.'

'Not bad for somebody who feels as daft as I do just now. Hang on for a moment.' She pulled some extraordinary faces.

'I'm with you now. Did you carry me over the bridge to the ambulance?'

'Yes. You do also remember that I moved in with you, for purely economic reasons?'

'Yes, of course.'

'Thank God for that. While they were pulling bits of glass out of you I've been busy letting people know that you won't be available until further notice.'

'That's what I was going to ask you to do.'

'Mr Holmes is looking after both dogs.'

'Great! I was worried about them.'

'He says that Dram's doing very well.' Roland judged that by now she was sufficiently *compos mentis* to cope with subjects requiring constructive thought. 'Do you want me to go on looking into the matter that we were investigating?'

'Oh, please do. I wouldn't want to let . . . whoever . . . get off with it just because I was stupid enough to go paddling in bare feet. I'll help all I can but it may not be much.'

'Start with this. I need to get about a bit. I'll probably have to keep coming up here to confer and it will take for ever if I have to hoof it everywhere or borrow a bicycle while trying to keep up with my own life and Simon's proofreading at the same time.'

'Use my car,' she suggested.

He blew out a breath of relief. 'That's what I hoped you'd say. So I brought your mobile for you to phone your insurers.'

'But the number . . .'

'I took it off the disc-holder on your windscreen.' He opened his hand and showed her some figures written on the palm in black Biro.

It took many minutes of argument and the telephone handset was getting hot before Roland became an authorized driver of Jane's car. There was an ominous mention of an additional premium but Jane waved it aside. 'By the time the bill comes in we should have got the rent money for your house. You'd better open my mail for me and pay any cheques into my current account, if we're so lucky. Then if you bring me up my chequebook I can let you have something for housekeeping. Am I sounding like a wife?' she asked anxiously.

'A little bit. I like it.' The words had slipped out before he was ready for them. He hurried to escape from such dangerous territory. 'Mr Holmes didn't recognize the description of the man in the tree. He said he'd think about it and look around.'

The nurse returned but Jane sent her away again. 'Well done,' she told Roland. 'You might also try my sister. You don't like her?' she added as Roland felt his face change.

'I feel intimidated by her, just as you do.'

'But you're a man.'

'I think men are more intimidated by women than other women are, but I'll try to be brave for your sake.'

'That's my hero in slightly rusty armour. When you see her, ask her again what it was that GG was going to tell me. And also, try to see Ross Grant. Ask him what naughty practices our common ancestor got up to. He was on the point of telling us when something interrupted him.'

At this point a nurse – a much more formidable specimen than her predecessor – arrived together with a porter and a trolley. Roland, she said, should have gone away long before and would he please remedy the omission forthwith. Miss Highsmith was being transferred for the moment to the New Royal Infirmary in Edinburgh.

Roland got up to go. With swift efficiency the nurse and the porter transferred Jane to the trolley. Roland wished her good luck and a swift recovery. Then, because she looked so lonely and afraid, he stooped quickly and kissed her on the lips. The nurse looked scandalized at such a flouting of elementary hygiene. As he drove down the hill he was remembering that kiss and trying to decide whether, as he hoped, there had been some response. Even a second or two of indignation would be better than the impression that she had not noticed.

FIFTEEN

Roland was too moved to look more deeply into Jane's problems that day. He settled his personal accoutrements into Jane's spare bedroom, made a simple meal which he was quite unable to taste and prepared for bed at an unusually early hour. He waited for as long as he could restrain himself before phoning the 'New Royal'. He was given to understand that Jane was waiting in a queue for a vacant theatre with the result that, as he lay awake, he was unable to rid his mind of a picture of Jane, still on the hospital trolley, awaiting her turn either in a queue of similar trolleys in a long hospital corridor or in a scene, dimly remembered from his teens, of a queue of wet mackintoshes below a poster heralding a musical comedy.

He slept at last, awoke feeling exhausted at around his usual time and roused himself by much use of cold water. He put off phoning the hospital because, though he knew it to be ridiculous, some corner of his mind insisted that he would be waking the hard-pressed hospital staff. This he soon recognized as his mind's way of postponing the dreaded moment when he must ask for news that might be unacceptable. People, he knew, did not always come out of the anaesthetic and hospitals could sometimes make terrible mistakes. When he could bear the suspense no longer he put aside a slice of toast with marmalade already spread on it and picked up the phone.

It took longer to track Jane to her ward than to assimilate the news, which was uniformly good. She had survived the anaesthesia. The surgeon who had completed the repairs to her foot was satisfied that the wound was clean and that all the nerves and blood vessels were correctly joined. If some superbug had found its way to the wound, despite the most rigorous efforts to exclude it, there was no sign of it yet. Roland brushed aside the statement that she was 'comfortable' – which may be said even of the deceased – but obtained assurances that she was sleeping naturally, might be able to accept a phone call that afternoon and if all went well would probably be returned to Newton Lauder the next day to relieve the eternally acute shortage of beds, which was made worse at that time by an out-of-season flu epidemic in Edinburgh and another epidemic in the provinces.

Roland whizzed round the house with the Dyson and mopped the kitchen. He answered the phone to a lady who was much troubled by a flatulent St Bernard and, out of his own past experience, directed her to the chemist for Windeze and to the pet food shop for a supply of granulated charcoal powder. Jane's morning mail proved to comprise unsolicited junk.

He was now free to do some writing on his own account, but he found that that part of his mind had gone unhelpfully blank. On the other hand, the cupboards and fridge were not well supplied. Jane's car was invitingly at the door and he knew that the tank was at least part full.

But first he walked round to his own house. The visitors were easily satisfied. His own mail looked more interesting than Jane's and indeed proved – *mirabile dictu!* – to contain a modest but welcome cheque in payment for an article that he had offered to a magazine some months earlier and quite forgotten.

With his mind made up for him he entered Jane's car, drove down the hill into Newton Lauder and parked in the Square. He paid an enjoyable visit to the bank, leaving his current account very slightly healthier but emerging with his wallet better filled than for several months past.

Almost next door was Kechnie's supermarket, a miniature version of the stores in bigger towns. He bought the immediate necessities. He then let impulse take over and, nerving himself to follow to the letter Jane's advice, haggled successfully with Mr Kechnie himself and bought luxuries. Jane, when she arrived home at last, was going to be indulged.

Another purchaser, evidently with a large family, had brought two cardboard cartons to the crowded checkout; the checkout assistant addressed him as Mr Adamson. Roland guessed his age as nearing fifty. He was as thin as

a bramble, possibly from the effort of keeping his family
in cereals. His features were bland apart from an over-
bearing nose, but his expression was malevolent. So this
was Mr Holmes's neighbour. Adamson put away his credit
card and picked up the first of his cartons leaving the other
beside the till. He pushed past Roland with only a glance
and no word of apology when he trod on Roland's foot,
but on his return journey he stopped, confronting Roland
and ignoring the tailback of shoppers gathering behind him.

'So you're the clown who's moved in with the vet girl,'
he said. 'And you're stirring up the shit.'

Roland was inclined to make allowances for any man encumbered by a hoard of children, but this was too much. Out
of the many possible ripostes that leaped to his mind he chose
what at the moment seemed to be the rudest and yet the most
innocuous. 'Have I stirred you up with the rest of it?'

Adamson did not miss the implication. 'What are you
calling me?' he demanded loudly.

Roland lowered his voice slightly. 'I didn't call you
anything; but if the cap fits, wear it.' Somebody nearby
suppressed a laugh.

Adamson's angular face darkened. He picked up his
second box and turned towards the doors. Roland kept
his toes out of harm's way.

The Terios was crawling back up the hill (because it was
far from new and had never been speedy uphill even in its
youth) when Roland realized that he had been too preoccupied with Jane's well-being to do anything about her
crusade. With fresh supplies in the car and even a small
renewed balance in the bank, he felt fit to slay dragons or
to beard fearsome ladies in whatever they considered to
be their dens. Instead of turning off to climb the precipitous
track to the rear entrance of Birchgrove he continued as
far as the hairpin bend and turned along the farm road.
The ruin of the cedar tree stood stark on the skyline,
reminding him of death. He parked at Whinmount, blocking
access to the garage, and rang the doorbell.

He had expected the formidable figure of Jane's sister,

dressed as he had last seen her in the guise of gracious hostess, or even a trim housemaid in cap and apron, but when Violet opened the door she was wearing an apron and had obviously been interrupted while doing the household chores. With a well practised sleight of hand, the apron and gloves vanished before the door was fully opened.

Violet seemed uncertain how to greet her sister's supposed boyfriend or whether or not to invite him inside. She compromised by saying, 'Good morning,' and then waiting for him to reveal his purpose.

''Morning,' Roland replied. He kept it brisk. 'I have some news for you about Jane.'

Violet looked as though she would have preferred to receive the news on the doorstep but her hand was forced. She invited Roland inside, led him into the kitchen and offered him both a chair and coffee. The room looked vast compared to those in Birchgrove. 'Forgive the kitchen,' she said. 'I haven't tidied the sitting room yet. I'm a bit short of time and I have an appointment with the dentist shortly. What about Jane?'

'We were fishing near here yesterday and she re-entered the stream barefoot. The sole of her right foot was very badly gashed by broken glass. She's undergone surgery in the Edinburgh "New Royal" and I'm told that she came through it well. She'll probably be brought back to Newton Lauder Cottage Hospital very soon. I'll keep you posted.'

'Thank you. And if I want more news, what's your phone number?' She reached for a pencil.

Roland should have anticipated that question but it caught him flat-footed. 'I . . . I'm staying in Jane's house at the moment,' he said.

'Oh?' The word was short but Violet's expression said it all – curiosity satisfied, superior amusement, sisterly delight, salacious interest. 'And how long has this been going on?'

He found himself blushing. 'Nothing is going on,' he retorted. 'Jane received an offer to rent her house for a few weeks but mine was more suitable for letting, so she lent me her spare bedroom.' To Violet's expression was added disbelief so he stumbled on. 'Jane wanted me to ask you a couple of questions.'

She glanced at her watch. 'Well, it doesn't seem that they can be about the birds and the bees. Ask away.'

Not unnaturally this comment made Roland's mind go blank. It took him several seconds to recall what was wanted. Then, when he tried to repeat Jane's version of how the man in the tree had been described to her, he was sure that the description was being garbled by repetition. Violet looked blank.

Roland gave up at last and switched to the second question. 'Jane says that just before GG went out that last time he said that he wanted to tell her something. Manfred suggested that it was about the money locked up in the house. She thought that you would probably know what it was about.'

Violet looked baffled but she was evidently thinking hard. 'GG never told me anything,' she said at last. 'He said that I talked when I should be listening, but who doesn't?'

'Not many people,' Roland agreed. 'But what had be been doing?'

'Been doing?'

Roland sighed. This was like trying to swim through cold porridge. 'Your great-grandfather,' he said, 'decided late at night that there was something that he wanted to say to Jane. There had to be a reason why he wanted to say it just then, rather late in the evening. It may have been something that he'd been thinking about all day, or something arising from what somebody'd said to him, or about something he'd found out. Had he had any letters or phone calls?' Violet shook her head slowly. 'But there must have been something. So I ask you again, what had he been doing? Who had he met? Where had he been?'

Violet's face was usually calm to the point of being secretive, but she took on a look of annoyance. 'If this is still about GG's death, can't you leave it alone? Tell Jane to accept the fact that he's gone and leave it at that.'

It seemed to Roland that all the intelligence in the family had been diverted in Jane's direction but he made up his mind to be patient and not in any circumstances to bark at her. Or to bite her in the leg, which was his other impulse.

'What GG said just then was probably the last thing that he said to anybody, ever. Doesn't that make it important?'

'I suppose it does.'

'So what was he doing on that last day?'

Violet's usually tranquil and comely face was again sullied by a frown. Evidently memory was an effort. 'He went down into Newton Lauder in the morning,' she said at last. 'To put petrol in his car – Jane's car now, of course. Then he spent some time in the attic. I remember that he took a camera up with him and I could hear him moving about but I've no idea what he was doing. That was in the afternoon. Then he sat down in his studio in that disgraceful old chair – I've thrown it out now, had to pay somebody to take it away would you believe? But he always said that it was the only comfortable chair in the house. He took his laptop on his knee – men aren't supposed to do that, are they? It's because they get hot underneath, but at his age you'd think that it wasn't important any more. I think he was only looking something up in Google and after that he was thinking, or else he fell asleep, or both.'

'Could he have been adding a codicil to his will?'

Roland saw her twitch but she answered firmly. 'Certainly not. For one thing, he'd have needed witnesses, wouldn't he? And now I'll have to ask you to go. I'm due at the dentist in ten minutes.'

She could surely delay for a few seconds. 'Could I just have a quick look at whichever camera he was using?'

It seemed that she was that great rarity, a woman who believed in arriving on time. 'Tomorrow,' she said firmly.

'Perhaps if I came back later—'

'We've been invited out. In the morning . . .'

So Roland found himself back in the car with his mind full of questions but sadly lacking answers. Was her behaviour suspicious? If somebody had consulted the Internet, was there a record of the subject? Had GG made any phone calls during those last few hours? He must insist on getting his hands on GG's computer. Roland was no expert but he knew that computers retained messages. Incoming emails in particular were duplicated on the bottom of replies. If he couldn't make it disgorge its information, he had a friend in Edinburgh who might be pressed into trying a little friendly persuasion.

SIXTEEN

Roland arrived back at Birchgrove to find that Jane's phone was ringing. In the strange manner by which telephones can communicate to a sensitive ear the degree of urgency by the manner of their ringing, he knew that it was a veterinary matter and quite beyond his capabilities. On the other hand he had become acutely aware that he had missed lunch and that if he had had any breakfast it had been before his memory had begun the day's record. This at least was something that he could ameliorate. He fried a leftover sausage with some bacon, two eggs and a slice of bread coated with cheese. The mushrooms still awaited attention so he peeled and chopped half of them and added them to the pan. After all, Jane had picked them so they should be all right.

He finished with a banana and a mug of coffee and, feeling much refreshed, turned his attention to the telephone. This had several times stopped and then resumed its ringing, expressing various degrees of urgency. It occurred to him that this might be the hospital with news of Jane or even summoning him to come and fetch her home. It proved, however, not to be a single call from a very determined caller but a succession of clients in need of veterinary help. Mr Hicks, it seemed, was unavailable and it fell to him to say so and to take a note, for the attention of Jane or Mr Hicks (whichever became available first) of the problems of a Siamese cat requiring a renewed prescription, a springer spaniel becoming seriously constipated and a golden retriever with what he recognized from a previous recollection of the near death experience of the family border terrier as incipient pyometra. This last he referred urgently to another vet some thirty miles away.

There was a certain pleasure to be found in pontificating to grateful pet owners about the maladies of their animals.

He wondered whether to study for a veterinary degree but, on the assumption that his relationship with Jane would continue, he remembered that books set against a veterinary background enjoyed a ready popularity. There was surely room in the market for a vet turned detective. Into his mind flashed a picture of a vet's assistant being attacked for the contents of the till but managing to implant a microchip in his/her masked assailant before losing consciousness.

The trickle of phone calls died away, which he took as a sign that Mr Hicks had returned to his surgery. He made contact at last with the errant vet and read him the now extensive list. In between times he had begun drafting a funny story about a bulldog who loved everybody except his doting owner. The working day was almost over. He polished the story and emailed it off to his chosen magazine.

He was in danger of nodding off. It had been a long and a busy day without, so far as he could recall, much being achieved. He made a milky drink and retired.

Too much was churning around in his mind. He was slow to fall asleep and then slept restlessly, falling at last into a deeper sleep so that he awoke considerably after his usual time. The telephone was ringing again as he stumbled down the stairs, still half asleep. He had had rather more than enough of the instrument and nearly ignored it. (He was one of the few people with sufficient detachment to ignore a ringing phone.) Grudgingly, he picked it up.

His mood improved and he was jerked above the interface between sleeping and waking by the sound of Jane's voice. She was back in Newton Lauder hospital and was allowed up on crutches but was forbidden to put her damaged foot to the floor – which, she said, she had not the least wish to do. It was soon clear that the object of the call was not to report on her recovery but arose out of either anxiety or curiosity as to how his enquiries were progressing.

'Not going very well,' he said. He paused for a yawn. 'I saw your sister. She didn't recognize the description of the man in the tree.'

'Or said she didn't.'

'Possibly,' he conceded, 'although I didn't see any signs of dissembling. I asked her what GG had been going to tell you and she began to give me an account of his last few hours, and I wanted to be shown the attic because he'd spent some time up there, but she was going out so she put me off until this morning. I also want to see his camera and his laptop.'

'And have you heard any more from Ian Fellowes?'

'Not a dicky bird.'

'I think you'd better come up and see me,' she said after a pause. 'This needs thinking about and talking over and there are people queuing up to use this phone.'

'I'll be up as soon as I've had some breakfast,' Roland said truthfully.

When he came to look in the fridge, Roland saw that it was well provided with the luxuries that he had bought for Jane's delectation but that he had made serious inroads into the more mundane foods such as one might take for breakfast. Cereals were in short supply. He had no idea how to make porridge. He seemed to have finished the bacon and all but one egg, but there remained a slice or two of bread, that single egg and, in a paper bag on the window sill, the remains of the mushrooms.

Before he had eaten more than half of his fry-up he began to feel far from well. His breathing, in particular, had become laboured. Immediately, association of ideas gave him a clue as to the cause. The mushrooms might mostly be perfectly edible but it would need only one or two poisonous fungi among them to produce his symptoms. He began to feel nauseous.

He kept his head, managing to drag rational thought up above the drugged confusion. His first impulse was to hurl himself into Jane's car and fly up to the hospital. But a sample would be wanted. There were several empty jars in the cupboard. He took samples, cooked and raw. He remembered the inconvenience of arriving in a hospital without personal possessions and he tossed his toiletries and some pyjamas

into a carrier bag. He put a new message on the answering
machine though he found that his voice was becoming thick.
Then he was ready. Although he was fumbling in his haste,
he managed to lock up carefully. Luckily the road from
Birchgrove to the cottage hospital is both short and unmis-
takeable. It was also empty. By now it needed conscious effort
to distinguish reality from hallucination. Despite confusion
of mind and vision he arrived safely, but walking across the
car park proved more difficult.

Newton Lauder is small as towns go, but it is the hub for a
number of villages and hamlets scattered through that part of
the Borders and so has more than the usual share of facilities. The cottage hospital would not have shamed a town three
times the size although it lacked a specialist and permanently
open A & E unit. Emergencies were rare and accidents were
dealt with as a matter of course or dispatched to Edinburgh.
The A & E function, Roland was aware, was covered by the
nurse on the main desk, who could summon available staff to
the two rooms dedicated to the purpose.

He was surprised, when he made his increasingly unsteady
way through the main doors, to find a scene of ordered but
intense activity. He was not to know that one of the local
milkmen had returned from a holiday in Europe bringing
with him the superbug *clostridium difficile* which he had
then distributed around his clients. The result was only now
making itself felt.

The nurse who seemed to be on desk duty turned away
from a small group which was conducting a debate in low
but vehement tones. 'Is it urgent?' she asked. She slapped
down an admission form in front of him. 'If not, you'll
have to wait or come back later.'

'I think it is urgent,' Roland said while scribbling. He
just knew that if he allowed this harpy to shunt him into a
siding he would be dead before anybody remembered him.
It took a huge effort to remember who he was, where he
was domiciled and how to spell the names while forming
the letters on the page. At the same time he forced his barely
controllable tongue to form other words. 'I'm sure I've

eaten some poisonous mushroom . . . fungus, toadstool . . . whatever. I think I'm going to . . .'

The nurse, who seemed used to such crises, took one look at his colour and produced a bowl out of nowhere. The bowl seemed to be made out of inferior papier mâché, but it served its purpose. One of the group of men broke off the argument and led him, vomiting, into a toilet. The man, a doctor to judge from the white coat and stethoscope, left him to void himself.

The group at the desk had now split, amoeba-like, into two. Half was continuing a medical discussion of infection control but Roland's doctor, the desk nurse and a gentle-looking lady whose badge declared her to be Senior Nursing Officer, were engaged in their own debate.

'This can't wait for analysis in Edinburgh,' said the doctor. 'For once, the patient's right, it's not *C.diff*, it's poisoning, it's urgent and we won't have a sterile ambulance spare until God knows when. Take him into a treatment room and see if you can get Dr Burns on the phone.'

'And what then?' demanded the SNO. 'We can't put him in with the *C diff* patients.'

'Lord, no! There's a vacant bed in with the girl with the cut foot,' said the doctor. He had a deep and gravelly voice. 'Designate that a two-bed mixed-sex high dependency ward.'

The SNO (who would earlier have been designated 'Matron') was old-fashioned and prepared to object, but the nurse piped up. 'He came in to visit her earlier. And, look, you can hardly read his writing but I think he was putting down the same address. So they're a couple.'

'All right,' said the SNO reluctantly. 'Put them in together.'

Roland, meantime, had been moved into a treatment room which sometimes served as a makeshift operating theatre. His head was swimming and he seemed to be drifting around the level of consciousness, sometimes above and sometimes below. He was aware that they had been joined by another doctor because he heard the gravelly voice say, 'This falls within one of your areas of interest. I'll leave you to it.'

The new doctor, soon confirmed as being Dr Burns, was

doing awful things to Roland while giving a running commentary – to himself or the nurse or possibly to Roland who was only aware of occasional words. 'No time to wait for analysis to come back . . . commonest toxins are arsenic, cadmium, copper and lead . . . don't be fooled if he seems better after a few days . . . liver is being damaged . . . have his samples gone?'

'The van was just leaving for Edinburgh when he came in,' said the nurse briskly. 'His samples went in with it, with a request for instant action and report. He brought cooked and raw samples with him.'

'Sensible chap. He may have saved himself from permanent damage.' Roland realized that there was an oxygen mask over his face. He dozed for what might have been a minute or an hour. '. . . done all we can . . . washed him out thoroughly . . . I'll phone and insist on an immediate report. I'll be back in my office . . .'

Roland was aware of yet another needle. He drifted deeper into unconsciousness.

Jane was brought back from having her wound examined and re-dressed. There were curtains around the other bed in her room and faint signs of life from beyond the curtains. So she was going to have company. A fellow patient might help to pass the time but would definitely inhibit discussion when Roland came to visit.

Three gowned figures arrived beside the other bed. 'These results,' said one of the two male figures, consulting an email, 'don't conform to any single poisonous fungus that I ever heard of, but I suggest that the present course of treatment remains the correct one. However, accidental ingestion of one or more poisonous fungi does not agree with the chemical facts. The only explanation I can come up with is that he has been subjected to deliberate poisoning with a mix of different fungi by someone who hoped that it would be put down to an accident with poisonous fungi.'

'Or an attempted suicide with the same end in view,' said the other male figure. 'Either way, the police will have to be informed. Nurse . . .'

'I'll notify them, shall I?' said the female figure.

'Yes. And then stand by in here until somebody comes.'

By now it had dawned on Jane that the newcomer was male. 'Are you putting a bloke in beside me?' she demanded.

'This is now a mixed sex high dependency ward. You have been rather out of things lately,' one of the doctors explained, 'so you may not know that we have had an outbreak of *C. diff.* Very dangerous, very unpleasant and subject to strict rules of segregation. This chap got the last vacant bed outside of the segregated wards. But we're quite accustomed to preserving the decencies in mixed sex wards so you need not fear for your modesty.' He returned his attention to the nurse. 'He's breathing for himself now. When you come back, try him without the oxygen but don't leave him alone.'

The nurse had been at school with Jane. 'Stay cool,' she said. 'He's in no condition to be a danger to you.'

'What the hell are you doing here?' Jane demanded.

Roland waited until he was freed from the oxygen and could speak without obstruction. 'Not my choosing,' he said thickly.

'I invited you to share my house but this is going too far.'

'Don't tell me, tell them. I just go where I'm put.'

'Mixed sex wards are quite normal these days,' said the nurse. 'And you each gave the same address. How were we to know?'

The question was unanswerable or rhetorical, possibly both. 'Anyway,' Jane said angrily, 'there was nothing wrong with those mushrooms when I picked them.'

Roland was recovering his wits. He spoke slowly, trying to be distinct. 'There was something bloody far wrong with something I ate,' he retorted, 'and the mushrooms are prime suspect, but I ate some of them last night and they did me no harm. Tell me, did you really think that I was going to invite a major session of vomiting, submit to being washed through and through with what was probably water but tasted like wrestler's socks, undergo jabs from dozens of needles, all of them large and none of them sharp, just so that I could be put to bed about as far from you as I was in your house?'

'Put like that,' Jane said more mildly, 'it does sound unlikely.'

'It does. Now shut up.'

Having made what almost amounted to an apology, Jane was hurt. 'You don't have to be like that about it. Be reasonable.'

'I am being reasonable. This is the only reasonable attitude. *Now* shut up.'

'Listening to you two carrying on,' said the nurse, 'anyone might mistake you for a married couple. You're both still half-doped.'

The police building is near the bottom of the hill on which the hospital stands and so it was only a matter of minutes before a plain clothes police sergeant arrived to stand guard. Roland was feeling sleepy and nauseous so he allowed himself to drift back into somnolence but Jane recognized Detective Sergeant Bright. She had once extracted a sharp bone from the anus of his basset hound. Bright was the right hand man of DI Fellowes who sometimes, in private, held him up as an example of ill naming. Bright was given to occasional feats of memory and sometimes moments of logical thought, but in general he seemed to be cogitating through a layer of treacle. He seated himself with no more than a nod and a word of greeting and opened his occurrence book on his knee, which was all that was needed to kill discussion dead. He had been told to stand guard and he had been trained to record everything, so those were the limits within which he was preparing to operate. He produced a football magazine and began to read.

Ian Fellowes arrived a few minutes later. He had brought Dr Burns in with him. The DI looked first at Jane. 'Your injury was accidental, is that correct?'

Jane, who had never considered any other possibility, took a millisecond to decide and agree.

'Right. Now somebody tell me why Mr Fox's mishap is a police matter. You are?'

'Dr Burns,' said the doctor. 'I'm a local practitioner. I was called in because I have an interest and some experience in cases of fungal poisoning. My first post-graduate appointment was in Ireland where we had a number of cases. Luckily for Mr Fox he had done the right things, I got to him early and the treatment that I had begun turned out to be correct. He had brought samples –' the doctor rattled the email that he was still carrying and which was becoming distinctly tatty '– which I sent in to Edinburgh with a demand for urgent analysis. The reply might have made sense if Mr Fox had ingested some of several different toxic fungi.'

The doctor paused, uncertain how to word the rest of his report. Fellowes helped him out. 'What you're saying is that for such a poisoning to happen accidentally would be almost incredible?'

'Delete almost and you've got it,' Burns said.

'Could the supposed mushrooms have been got at by an outsider?'

The last draught of a milky liquid seemed to have settled Roland's nausea for the moment but he was still exhausted and his mind seemed clouded. He had heard what was being said without bothering to understand it, but he now realized that he was being addressed. He made a vaguely interrogatory noise and Fellowes repeated the question. Roland examined his misted memory. 'Yes,' he said at last. 'They were in a bowl in the kitchen on the window sill and the window was unlatched because I'd been frying things.' He climbed a little higher out of the mental mire. Jane was emitting clouds of disapproval. 'I know,' he said. 'Frying is bad for you, grilling is better. But I *like* a fry-up now and again.'

'So do I,' said the doctor. 'But I restrain myself. I'll be available,' he added to the DI and he turned on his heel and left the room.

Fellowes' eyes followed the receding back as though he would have liked to fetch the doctor back by the scruff of his neck. Instead, he grunted and returned his eyes to Roland. 'Can you think of any reason why anybody might want to kill or incapacitate you, other than your enquiries into the death of Mr Grant?'

Roland had allowed himself to subside into the fringes of sleep. He decided that he could not think of anything at all. 'Tell you later,' he said.

DI Fellowes managed not to swear aloud, but he was inwardly furious. These two would have to remain in hospital and under guard. The continuous presence of an officer would require three men in shifts. He only had three men. Common sense suggested that, unless he could borrow from the uniformed branch, he would have to refer to Edinburgh, which would undoubtedly result in the arrival of somebody more senior to assume command. He would have preferred to assume that the poisoning of Roland Fox could just possibly have been accidental, but if that left the door open for another and successful attempt on Roland's life the consequences to himself would be almost as severe and to Roland would be worse.

Roland, meanwhile, had opened one eye and found that one of Jane's eyes was meeting his. They yawned in unison. ''secutor,' Roland mumbled. Jane made a noise that he took for assent.

SEVENTEEN

The ensuing week dragged by with the ponderous slowness of a year. Jane hobbled into the bathroom and back on crutches while Roland, once he was pronounced out of danger though still very shaky, had the use of sticks as an alternative to a zimmer. This returning mobility was of no great benefit to them. The *C.diff* infection in the rest of the hospital meant that they were strictly confined to their room. The need for daily dressing of Jane's wound and constant monitoring of Roland's organs prevented their discharge. With exercise so limited they found it difficult to keep joints and muscles working despite the visits of the physiotherapists.

Visitors were rare. They put this down to the presence of *C.diff* only just beyond the nearest partition. The infection seemed to have replaced satanic visitation in the public consciousness.

A welcome visitor late that week was Mr Enterkin. The solicitor, now a very old man but still agile of mind, was the executor of GG's will. His formal suit was obviously new but old-fashioned in style. He entered, leaning on two sticks but with a smile perceptible on his age-raddled face, and arranged himself comfortably in a visitor's chair. 'I met young Ian Fellowes,' he said. 'He tells me that you're very anxious for a word with me.'

'As you would have known if you ever listened to your messages,' Roland said.

The solicitor waved a dismissive hand. 'I would have done so, given time. I have been busy, very busy. Lord Hawburn's lawsuits, about which you may have read, are now settled. I don't know what all the hurry is about. If it's the Grant executry, you must know that these things take time. Yes, indeed. For the moment, no beneficiary is suffering.'

'*I* am suffering,' Jane said. 'I am living hand to mouth.'

'When you hear the terms of the will—'

'I have been waiting several weeks –' Roland was aware that trying to hurry a lawyer only allows time to dribble away but Jane was not so trammelled '– and there is another reason to get a move on,' she said. 'You know that there are questions as to whether GG's death was accidental?'

'So Inspector Fellowes informed me. He intended to join us, by the way, but I have just received a phone call to say that he will be delayed until this afternoon. He is very anxious to bring the details in Mr Grant's will and the trust into the open, to clear up any questions of motivation. Personally I find it hard to believe—'

Jane, who had been lounging on the side of her bed, sat up suddenly. 'Trust? What trust? Is this to do with Wyvern Grant's paintings? But they're rubbish. Aren't they?'

Mr Enterkin seemed unflustered. 'I am in no position to comment. I know nothing about art values and have never seen the paintings. Indeed, I am not sure where they are nor whether they are the subject of the trust.' Each of his listeners showed signs of interrupting but the solicitor held up a hand to signify that he still had the floor. 'In England it would be normal at this stage to read the will in the presence of the beneficiaries and anybody else affected. In Scotland it is less universal but very convenient to follow the same procedure. I considered doing so in here, but on my way in I broached the matter with the Senior Nursing Officer. In view of the present risk of hospital-borne infection, she felt reluctant to relax the rules about visitor numbers. Instead, she suggested that you are both doing well and a venture into the outside world might do you good. Given a little help from the hospital staff you could be brought to Whinmount and returned again to the hospital without harm. If that is suitable I could call a meeting at Whinmount for, say, two thirty?'

Roland, who had been looking forward to the first excuse to stretch his legs out of doors, could see no objection. Jane, however, had no intention of being seen in her old home by her sister and others including a former lover, in the bloodstained jeans and jumper in which she had been admitted nor in a dressing robe and hospital gown. She agreed in principle but then sent a panic message to her school friend among the nurses and persuaded her to visit Birchgrove and to bring back the nearest to suitable clothes that she could find.

Shortly before two thirty, the converted ambulance that was usually given over to the transport of outpatients to and from specialist clinics in Edinburgh stopped at the Whinmount steps. Roland was the first to alight. His knees felt distinctly wobbly after a period of disuse but he turned to steady Jane in her one-legged descent. However, there was a porter present for that purpose and Roland could only take Jane's crutches while the porter half-carried her up the five steps. In his own turn, Roland found that the knack of walking returned quickly but that the strength in the knees required for climbing steps was another matter. He caught up at the door, puffing slightly. Other cars were grouped in front of the garage.

Violet, very much the hostess in a well chosen dress both new and expensive, took them into the sitting room. An effort had been made to give the room a welcoming look, with a log fire in the grate and flowers on the tables. Mr Enterkin was already established in the most comfortable armchair. Ross Grant was on his feet and studying through a magnifier a painting of kittens playing around a vase of flowers. Ian Fellowes had seated himself in a corner and was pretending to be invisible.

Room was made for the two convalescents on the settee. When the chatter had subsided, Mr Enterkin assumed control by force of personality without, so far as Roland could remember, uttering a sound.

'I requested this meeting,' the solicitor said, 'in order to clarify the matters in the will of Mr Luke Grant and to obtain certain relevant information.

'As some of you may be aware, the will is encumbered by a very old trust originated by his ancestor Wyvern Grant, an artist whose career overlapped the eighteenth and nineteenth centuries. But we will come to that later. Let us first consider the will itself.'

The solicitor had a fat wad of papers on his knee but he spoke entirely from memory and without referring to them. 'After settlement of debts and expenses, any cash or similar assets are to be divided equally between his two great-granddaughters. Apart from his earnings he seems to have been living on annuities, so this is unlikely to amount to much; indeed, after deductions there may even be a negative balance.' (Jane subsided with a grunt.) 'Income from future sales of his work, which is still in frequent demand for cards, calendars and illustrations for books and magazines, will also be equally divided.

'As I think you know, all his photographic equipment – cameras, printers and including his computers and filing cabinets – are left to Mrs Violet Young. Anything of a recreational nature and in particular his fishing tackle and associated material is left to Jane Grant, now to be known again as Jane Highsmith. This includes any car or cars in his ownership.'

Violet frowned and jerked upright. 'He only kept a car in order to get around his photographic commitments,' she snapped.

'The legacy is clearly spelled out,' said the solicitor. 'He was aware that you had a car but Miss Jane did not. That will have been the reasoning.'

Violet subsided. Roland wanted to ask her whether she would really have deprived her sister of the car that would be essential to the launch of her career while she, Violet, already had a newer, bigger and shinier one, but he decided to save the question for later. There would undoubtedly be more battles to come when such a barb might prove useful.

'This house, known as Whinmount, together with all the associated gardening and housekeeping tools and machinery but excluding domestic furniture and other contents are to be considered a single legacy,' the solicitor continued. 'Minor personal items may be divided between you by agreement but in the event of disagreement I am to act as arbiter. This legacy, the house and its contents, is bequeathed to Mrs Young in the first instance. But there are certain conditions.'

'We know about those,' Violet said impatiently. 'GG told me. There has to be a home available for my sister for as long as she wants it. Jane has moved out and made it perfectly clear that she prefers to live in the house that was left to her by our step-great-grandmother. I think that deals with that.'

Mr Enterkin looked at her curiously. 'That was the only condition about which your great-grandfather advised you?'

Violet froze, lost colour and then managed to nod.

'The other condition might not have seemed relevant at the time,' said the solicitor, 'but I must quote it now. Mrs Young's possession of this house takes the form of a life rent. It is conditional on her living in it as her principal and permanent residence, failing which owner-ship reverts to her sister, Jane. The exclusion of furniture from this legacy is because Jane already has furniture. The furniture is left to Mrs Young absolutely.'

For a moment Roland thought that somebody had left the room. Then he realized that the sudden absence was of sound. The hush was total. When Violet broke the silence it was in a voice that had risen by most of an octave. 'I consider that iniquitous,' she squeaked. 'Surely he can't make a gift like that and then snatch it back?'

'I'm afraid he can,' said the solicitor.

Roland was less concerned with the distant future than with present implications. 'If you really want to move,' he said, 'you should be in a position to re-house yourselves. You have two incomes. Why are you so concerned?'

'None of your damn business!' Violet snapped. Manfred put a hand on his wife's arm but she shook it off. 'I've already consulted Mr Enterkin about my reason but he said nothing about this condition. This is not supposed to be announced yet so we were holding it for a surprise. But we – Manfred and I together – have been offered a dream job in Dublin at salaries we can't afford to refuse. Such an offer will never come again – there is only one firm of developers big enough to need the in-house services of top-notch photographers and model makers.'

'Though we say it ourselves,' Roland whispered audibly.

He was ignored. 'There's a house comes with the job but we'd have to buy it.'

'So buy it,' Roland said.

'But we'd have to get a mortgage if we didn't have this house to sell,' Violet said, stating what she considered to be an insuperable objection.

Roland was about to ask why a mortgage would be such a disaster for Violet when it was the norm for most of the rest of humanity. Jane forestalled him. 'If I inherit this house,' she said, 'I'll be able to sell mine. Then I can lend you some money. Half what I get for my house. There!'

'Interest free?' Violet asked quickly.

Jane hesitated. A discussion both endless and acrimonious seemed imminent. Roland said, 'I suggest free of interest for five years and thereafter interest at the prevailing bank rate.'

'Agreed.'

Jane nodded and sat back, relieved that boundaries had been set to her impetuous offer. Such generosity towards one who had just attained the pinnacle of selfishness had taken Roland's breath away. It seemed to have much the same effect on Manfred, who changed colour several times but remained silent, and even on Jane herself.

The solicitor was not so easily silenced. 'When you first consulted me about the details of the Irish contract, I was virtually certain that you would opt for Ireland and leave this house to your sister. I was not free to advise you of that clause at the time.'

'Why not?' Violet almost screamed.

'Because your great-grandfather had not yet confirmed his intention. You'll appreciate that the remainder of this meeting depends mostly on which option you choose. It would hardly be equable to allow you to retain possession for an unspecified period before abandoning it. I therefore took the liberty of preparing a paper for your signature, confirming that you do not intend to retain possession of this house and agreeing to payment of a reasonable rental if you do not vacate this house within six months.'

'I'll sign it,' said Violet. Her face had paled so that her makeup stood out unnaturally. 'I'm not going to give up the Irish job and we couldn't possibly commute from here. Give it to me.' She took the page of legal paper and held out her hand to her husband.

Manfred hesitated and then reluctantly handed over a fountain pen. 'Perhaps you should wait until you have heard about the trust,' he said.

Violet's voice rose again. 'That trust! I'm sick of hearing about it and never seeing anything that's covered by it. If there is anything in it, I'm sure it's not worth a row of beans. It may be a painting or a rude limerick by Robert Burns, I don't want to know.' Violet scrawled a signature and then jumped to her feet. 'Manfred and I are going to Dublin for the rest of the week. That will let us firm up the other house in the same visit. We'll be committed,' she pointed out to Jane, 'so I'll hold you to your offer. You made it in front of witnesses, remember.'

'I remember,' Jane said. 'There's no need to get in a tizzy about it. I don't go back on my promises.'

Her last words were addressed to a closed door. Violet had left the room, drawing a reluctant Manfred with her.

'We will attach witness signatures,' Mr Enterkin said composedly, 'and then we can get down to other business. Before we deal with the trust, perhaps I should explain that I invited Mr Ross Grant to be with us, partly because he has some specialized knowledge but also because he is a beneficiary in a small way. He has a number of books, documents and photographs on loan and these are bequeathed to him absolutely.

'Now perhaps we can move on.

'I was appointed trustee by the Court of Session,' said the solicitor, 'on the death of my predecessor and, I believe, solely on the grounds of geographic propinquity. I have glanced over the documents and that is the limit of my knowledge and understanding to date. The original documents are couched in archaic legalese which even I was sometimes hard put to it to interpret. The gist of it is that an ancestor of Luke Grant, and therefore of yourself, Miss Highsmith, was a painter, Wyvern Grant. He was an eccentric character but well acquainted with the great men of his time – for instance, rather than pay a lawyer to draft the documents he seems to have persuaded the then lord advocate, whose portrait he had painted, to assist him.

'Wyvern Grant must have had an exaggerated opinion of his own talent as a painter. Throughout the text there is evident a querulous belief that he was a misunderstood genius – this despite the fact that he seems to have enjoyed some small degree of success in his lifetime. He moved among the great men of his day and seems to have believed his own talent superior to theirs.'

'Which I presume it was not,' Roland said.

Ross Grant made a face expressive of disgust. 'Very definitely not. He was a moderately competent draughtsman who had picked up a number of facile tricks to create a quick impression of . . . let's call it *sparkle*. If you study any one of his few surviving paintings you may like it at first glance but after a few minutes it seems tawdry.'

Roland was struck by a coincidence of ideas. 'When we met here for dinner,' he said to Ross, 'you began to tell us that Wyvern was a man with some undesirable habits. You were interrupted before you could go into any detail. Were you about to tell us that among those habits was one of purloining the work of others?'

Ross nodded. He seemed to be blossoming while his expertise was being deferred to. 'He is mentioned in the autobiographies of several of his contemporaries, and never in very flattering terms. It was generally agreed that his talent was for self-promotion. He felt that the world owed him the materials with which to exhibit his skill. Any fellow artist careless enough to leave a canvas, whether blank or painted, where Wyvern could get his hands on it might well not see it again, or not to recognize it.'

'Ah!' said Enterkin. 'Now some of the provisions in the trust begin to make sense. His collection – unspecified –

was left in trust to the most senior of his male descendants, to be retained in the family but available for exhibition or for study by students or historians. If the male line should die out, the trust ceases to have effect and the collection may be sold.'

'How many in the male line are left?' Jane asked.

'That was the question that I asked myself as soon as I heard of the death of your great-grandfather. While I busied myself untangling the affairs of the unfortunate Lord Hawburn I engaged the services of a genealogical researcher. There was provision in the will for such expenditure. The answer is none. There seems to have been a genetic bias towards the distaff side.'

'Allow me to point out,' Ross Grant put in, 'that I am a male Grant descended from Wyvern Grant.'

'Perfectly true,' Mr Enterkin said. He tapped the papers on his knee. There was about him a trace of smug triumph. 'But it was your great-grandmother who was descended from Wyvern and she married another Grant who was no relation.'

Jane was frowning, afraid of leaping to a conclusion. 'Then the collection may now be sold? And the proceeds divided between us?'

Enterkin shook his head. 'Yes and no. Perhaps I should have mentioned a condition that the collection was to be kept in this house when not on loan for exhibition. If sold, the proceeds go to the owner of this house.' He paused and looked Jane in the eye. 'Since your sister signed the transfer document, that is you.'

Jane appeared dumbstruck. Roland said, 'So Jane is now free to sell something, we're not sure what and have no idea of its value and we don't even know where it is and might not recognize it if we came across it?'

'Succinctly put,' said Mr Enterkin, 'but accurate. The only clue that I can add is that the original deed has a pencilled one-word annotation in one margin. This has become slightly smudged over the years but it seems to consist of the word *trap*. And now I must leave you. I have another meeting in –' he glanced at his watch '– less than

twenty minutes. It was my duty to clarify the legal position. The nature and location of the legacy is another matter.'
He struggled to his feet, made gracious farewells all round
and left the room.

EIGHTEEN

Roland was the first to break the silence. 'Do you still want to find this legacy?' he asked Jane. 'The verdict of history seems to be that it's valueless. We could expend a lot of time that could be better spent pursuing our careers and find either nothing or something of no value, or even something that we'd rather not know.'

'That seems a sensible view,' said Ross.

Jane was looking thunderous. 'Yes we bloody well do want to find it, whether it's valuable or not. You're forgetting the probability that it had something to do with GG's death. We must search, using our brains. The attic is the most likely place.'

'In that case, what are we to make of the word *trap?* Does it mean to beware of a trap wherever the whatever-it-is is hidden?' said Roland. 'Or that there is some intention to mislead? Or even that there is something dangerous within the text or other material?' There was no comment. 'You said once that he'd just made a phone call,' he reminded Jane.

They both looked at Ross, who shrugged. 'Not to me,' he said firmly.

'In that case,' Jane began. She paused and was seen to be thinking deeply. Roland wanted to help her but he had no idea where her mind was going. 'You may be able to help us a lot at a later stage,' she said at last to Ross, 'but for the moment I think you should leave us.'

Ross hesitated, looking displeased. He seemed about to protest but he rose, nodded a farewell to each of them and left the room. They heard the front door close and a car drive off.

'Perhaps my presence has also become *de trop*,' Ian Fellowes said. 'I only attended in order to hear the terms of the will.'

He began to get up but Jane leaned forward, put a hand on his arm and gently pushed him back. He settled in his chair with a faint smile and Roland guessed that he had had no intention of leaving but of preparing to tell a court, *I was present at the request of the householder*. 'Oh, no you don't,' Jane said. 'I said that the attic is the most likely place. Can you see me climbing ladders, one legged? Or Roland, for that matter?' Roland could have felt offended, but remembering his own image in his shaving mirror that morning he had to admit to himself that he looked as he felt, twice his age and feeble with it.

'I don't do my own climbing any more,' Ian Fellowes said, 'and certainly not without witnesses standing by.' He produced his radio.

'Wait,' Jane said. 'We won't have time to do much searching in what's left of the day. And Ross Grant has the reputation of being the biggest chatterbox for miles around. By dusk, half the region will know that there's probably something in the attic worth stealing and that Violet and Manfred are going to Dublin.'

'But they won't know when,' Roland said. He pushed himself to his feet and half-walked half-hobbled to the door. He found Violet depositing a suitcase in the hall. Violet was sullen. He thought that she was mentally picking over the recent discussion and wondering whether she had been diddled – or had diddled herself. 'We're going in an hour or so,' she said. 'That way we can catch the most suitable flight.'

Roland returned to the sitting room. 'They're leaving soon.'

'We're expected back at the hospital,' Jane said. 'My wound has to be dressed and Roland's due his medication. We don't want some tearaway running off with Robert the Bruce's jockstrap or whatever it's going to turn out to be. Somebody's going to have to stay on guard.' She produced a grin that was balanced somewhere between amusement and mischief. 'I am notifying you before witnesses, Detective Inspector Fellowes, that I have reason to believe that a break-in will shortly be attempted at this house and

I look to you for some sort of protection. Unless, of course, you feel that it's a matter for the uniformed branch?'

Ian Fellowes had been sitting, speaking very little, unmoving except to make an occasional note. He set his jaw. 'I do indeed. But I don't see them lending me at least one constable for overnight duty on the slender grounds that we've seen so far. However, I have had one youngster on loan and I could stretch his secondment a little longer. He's eager for a transfer to CID.'

'That's settled,' Jane said. 'We'll meet again in the morning.'

The DI straightened up and locked eyes with Jane. 'You have no grounds for believing that whatever, if anything, is up there has something to do with your great-grandfather's death,' he said.

Jane looked at him much as she might have looked at a nasty case of parvo virus. 'I didn't say that I was sure, only that there was a high probability. I still want to know what happened to GG and this seems to be the best starting point that we have. And I'll tell you something else. During this last week, GG's last days have been in my mind. He spent a lot of time up in the attic. Well, when we were young, Vi and I with a few local friends used to play hide and seek all through the rest of the house. Several small girls looking for hiding places would hardly have missed a space large enough to hold several paintings, even rolled up, if that's what it's all about. But until a few years ago you could only get into the attic by a way of a heavy trap door and a ladder that was kept out in the shed. We never managed to go up there; later, GG had the proper sliding loft ladder installed and a roof light put in.

'And you must know how things come back to you when you're in bed and half asleep, on the frontier between thought and dreaming. While I was waking up this morning, the last time that I saw GG came into my mind. I'd had a vague idea that the last words he said to me had been to the effect that there was a lot of money . . . cash . . . somewhere in the house. Then I thought that he meant that there was a lot of value tied up in the property. But it came back to me quite clearly. He said that there was something valuable in the house. I think he said "hidden". Then he said that he'd have to speak to Mr Enterkin about it.'

'Changing his will, you think?' Fellowes asked.

'I never even thought of that, so if you're hinting that I might have had a motive . . .'

Ian Fellowes seemed genuinely stumped. 'That had honestly never occurred to me. And I don't think we'll do more than bear it in mind as a remote possibility. The fact that the death would have passed as accidental but for your activities goes a long way towards clearing you.'

Jane was prepared to compromise. 'But he could have been changing his will, if he'd just realized that what he had to leave was more valuable than he'd thought, or that the conditions of the trust were affected.' She shook her head. 'It's no good beating our brains out – we just don't have enough data. We must search. Then if we find anything, or if we don't, at least we have something to think about and a basis to start from.'

Ian Fellowes produced his radio again. Further discussion was cut off by the return of the converted ambulance and a ring at the doorbell. Roland found that his outing had tired him but he paused in the hall to say, 'I take it that the attic is full of junk, like every other attic I know?'

'Possibly not!' Jane said. 'I believe it has a lot of stuff in it but whether or not it's junk only time will tell. Treasures have often been found among the forgotten items in people's attics.'

'I wasn't thinking of value. I was wondering whether we'd be able to get around it and search.'

Back at the cottage hospital they found the staff confused and harassed by the arrival of three more sufferers from *C.diff*. The Edinburgh hospitals, it appeared, were declining to relieve the pressure by accepting the overflow from Newton Lauder because of the risk of introducing the infection and the great difficulty of keeping it localized. Even so, the local doctors were reluctant to allow Jane and Roland to be walking wounded again on the morrow. Only when

Roland accused them of becoming fixated on looseness of the bowels and Jane compared them to cats that had caught two mice, and then only when the SNO intervened, was agreement reached.

When they were in their separate beds and the curtain had been drawn back again, Roland took a careful look to be sure that they were alone and said, 'One thing I don't understand. Mr Enterkin gave your sister no warning that in giving up the house to you she was also giving up any claim on the trust. That doesn't seem very even-handed to me.'

'Perhaps it wasn't,' said Jane. 'But she didn't believe in the trust anyway. Even now we don't know that there's anything of value in the trust.'

'But there could be. He should have warned her.'

'Perhaps he should but he didn't. Please, Roland, leave it at that.'

There was a long silence until Roland suddenly said, 'I'm sorry, but we're trying to investigate a mystery and one of the few things we have to follow up is when somebody does something out of pattern. Enterkin's strange reticence on the subject has to be noted as odd behaviour.' He could have added that Jane's own attitude was no longer what he had believed to be her norm. To say so aloud might prejudice his relationship with her, but not to speak out might leave him faced with a long hunt while he had doubts about the innocence of one who might be considered his client.

There was another, shorter, silence while Jane pondered whether to reveal the secret. 'I'd better tell you,' she said at last. 'Otherwise you'll blurt out the wrong thing at the wrong moment and to the wrong people. And I'll never forgive you or speak to you again if you ever mention it or back Violet up if she decides to make a case of it. That's if she ever realizes that she's been had, which I find unlikely. Her mind's too full of the career break and the new house and my loan. But if you really want to know, Mr Enterkin is my Godfather.'

'That's naughty,' Roland said after a thoughtful pause.

*   *   *

The two, after their outing, had slept well and awoke with appetites refreshed. They were coping with the early hospital breakfast when the first message reached them. DI Fellowes would appreciate their attendance at Whinmount as soon as would be practicable. The SNO pointed out that the Patient Transport vehicle was already on its way to Edinburgh and that any ambulance that could possibly be spared would not have been decontaminated. Ian Fellowes, not to be thwarted, sent a police Range Rover to fetch them; and this was under the command of a tough, uniformed sergeant who would accept no interference, considering doctors to be only one step removed from repair mechanics and as dust beneath his wheels.

At Whinmount, Jane was lifted carefully out of the adjusted front seat and carried up the steps by the same sergeant. Inside, they found a scene of what could only be considered confused calm. An overalled man, who Jane recognized as a retired policeman who had retrained as a SOCO, was examining the area around the loft ladder while Ian Fellowes and DS Bright stood by, miming helpfulness but unable to make a contribution. Jane and Roland were confined to the ground floor and offered at first only a barely coherent account of what had occurred. It was only the return of a panda car with Ian's other two constables that offered an explanation. The young officer who had remained on guard duty had been found an hour earlier, battered and barely conscious. He had been sent to Edinburgh by ambulance in case of serious brain damage and the DI had sent a PC with him to gather as much information as possible. The panda car had followed the ambulance to bring the accompanying PC and his report back.

That report had hardly been worth the extra mileage. The young aspirant to CID status had been dozing in a chair below the trap door concealing the loft ladder when he had realized that a dark figure was looming over him. He had then been felled by a single blow to the head. The SOCO, who had reached the scene before the ambulance arrived, suggested that the weapon had been a china rolling pin from the kitchen which was found near the head of the stairs, happily unbroken. The SOCO had collected a great many samples but whether any of them would ever prove to be of use was not yet clear. The front door remained locked but the sash-and-case kitchen window had proved to be an easy point of entry.

With the preliminaries over, the scene could now be opened up and Jane and Roland allowed up the stairs.

The attic turned out to be a single long rectangle covering the whole house, floored and lined with heavy pitchpine boarding. As was to be expected in a very old house, the attic had been used as a repository for many years and not all the deposits had ever been removed. A dozen and more boxes including chests, tea boxes, an old trunk and several cardboard cartons were stored there but the contents had been flung on the floor by the night's intruder and so mingled that it was far from clear what each box had contained.

A system was soon developed. DSgt Bright, supervised by Ian Fellowes, picked up each item and restored it to whichever box seemed to be the most appropriate. A description was relayed by Roland, who had dragged his way to the top of the ladder, to Jane below who was struggling to maintain a sensible list. Nothing whatever was found that could be described as treasure or have warranted the establishment of a trust, although some items of damaged silverware and a badly scratched marquetry box were set aside for expert attention. They found outmoded clothes, including souvenirs of GG's athletic triumphs from before his war wound, all reeking of camphor and other mothproofing. There were forgotten toys, framed photographs of equally forgotten relatives and a whole box of superseded household tools. Many of these might have attracted the interest of a collector.

Late in the morning, they finished the first sift through the boxes and broke off for a snack meal. Just then there came news from Edinburgh. The injured constable had serious concussion but would make a good recovery thanks to an unusually thick skull. But he had no more recollection of events prior to the attack. A message was sent back along the same route, saying that his recollections were to be reported as soon as his memory began to improve.

'Thank God for that!' Jane said. 'His condition, I mean. I would never have forgiven myself if he'd been permanently handicapped or even killed.' She bit into a biscuit and cheese. It had been generally agreed that any food in the house must have been included with Jane's legacy and Jane had put together a simple meal which they were consuming, picnic style, while they talked.

Roland looked up at the ceiling. 'I've been thinking about the word *trap*,' he said. 'Enterkin mentioned that it had been pencilled in a margin of the trust document. The only trap I can see is the hole the loft ladder comes through. But Wyvern Grant had been dead for many years before that trap door was made.'

'Not quite so,' Ian Fellowes said. 'The loft ladder was comparatively recent but a hole must have been there to give access and there are no signs that it's been altered.'

DSgt Bright had bolted a sketchy meal and had been pottering about, wandering apparently at random. 'May I say something?' he asked suddenly. It seemed that he had been slapped down so often by Ian Fellowes that he was afraid to put himself forward.

Ian nodded. 'Go ahead.'

The DSgt was toying with a small round container from which emerged about two metres of steel measuring tape. An untidy bunch of papers hung from his pocket. 'I'm no architect,' Bright said, 'but I thought I'd check the size of the building. If something's hidden, the space has to come from somewhere.'

'That's reasonable. What did you find?' Jane asked him.

'In most cases,' Bright said carefully, 'the distance from the edge of the trap to the inside of the outside wall – you understand?' he interposed anxiously.

'We understand,' Fellowes said. 'Get on with it.'

'It was the same in the attic and the first floor, except for perhaps an inch or so, not enough to count. Of course, the front and back of the roof slope, so it's difficult to measure but that isn't where you'd hide something – blocking off a secret cupboard would be too obvious. It's at the upright gable end walls that you could cut off some space. The distance from the edge of the trap door to the back of the shower compartment on this floor corresponds exactly with the measurement in the attic from the trap to the inside of the gable in the attic. But taking the same measurement in the opposite direction, to the back of the wardrobe, there's a difference of about six hundred millimetres, say two feet. It's the loft that's shorter, not this floor.'

There was a moment of silence broken by the sound of stirring interest, a catch of breath, an interrogatory murmur, the shuffle of a foot. 'So there's a vacant space walled off. Can you open it up?' Jane asked.

'Not without damage,' Ian said. 'We'd better get a joiner.'

'You won't get one before tomorrow morning,' Jane said. 'And he'd still have to do damage. Are you going to leave somebody else on guard and find him clonked on the head in the morning? There's a crowbar in the shed. It's my house now and I shan't mind about damage to the linings of the attic.'

'Only one board need be much damaged,' Roland pointed out. 'Get one board out and you can push or knock the others out from behind.'

'That seems reasonable,' Ian said. 'Bright, this was your inspiration so the honour's yours. Fetch the crowbar.'

Bright flushed with pleasure and hurried downstairs. He was back with the crowbar within seconds. Ian Fellowes went up with him. Roland was nearing exhaustion but he hauled himself up to sit in the trap. As Roland had suggested, one board suffered badly but after that it was easier. When he had three boards out, Bright reached into the gap and drew out a frame with canvas tacked across it.

'It isn't as dusty as I'd expected,' Ian said.

'What is it?' Jane demanded from the floor below. 'Come on! Tell me, dammit!'

'I was just about to tell you,' Roland said. 'You really must learn to curb your impatience. You surely didn't think that I was going to keep you in ignorance while I held in my hands the answer to all the questions we've been asking each—'

'All right,' Jane said. '*All right!* I'm sorry. Now will you please tell me what the hell it is?'

Roland relented. 'It's a painting in oils, canvas on a wooden stretcher, depicting a man in pre- or early-Victorian evening dress. The colours are vivid and not very well handled and the gentleman seems to have a slight squint. Also he's slightly off-balance. Frankly, it looks more than a little bit amateurish. It has the initials WG in the corner and a small label reads Hon Josiah Dunn. There are a lot more paintings in here and I'll hand them down to you if you want to collect them down there.'

'Do that,' said Ian Fellowes. 'They'll have to be in safe custody until we've worked out what all the fuss is about. Somebody list them. Tomorrow we can bring back Ross to add his more expert opinion.'

'Which,' said Roland, 'we may take with the proverbial pinch of salt.'

NINETEEN

Before they left for the night, the hidden space at the end of the attic was examined in more detail and it was found that there were no less than 68 paintings, some of them small but others designed to embellish some huge hall or ballroom. The sheer volume would have made removal into secure storage a major undertaking, so Ian Fellowes again left a man on duty, this time the eager DSgt Bright. It may be that Bright was chosen because Ian had a conscious or subconscious hope that another visitor might rid him of a subordinate who, however keen, was too often a thorn in his flesh, but there were no alarms during the night and the DSgt, who had become caught up in the mystery, forewent his right to time off in lieu and was present at Whinmount when a police liveried Range Rover again brought Jane and Roland to the door. This time, Ross Grant's neat Audi arrived almost on their heels.

Bright had been busy. With unusual thoughtfulness he had brought several folding chairs to the landing beneath the trap so that at least the two invalids could be seated; and he had brought all the paintings, some on canvas and some on boards, down from their cache. These were arranged along the skirting and the picture rail of the landing and took up the whole double length of both sides. There were also two battle scenes on large canvases which had been rolled up and defied most efforts to hold them flat. At a first glance, Roland was less than impressed. The daubs looked amateurish even to his untutored eye but were distinguished from the works of other painters by a certain vividness of colour and exaggeration of tone that might well have convinced an unsophisticated artist of his own genius. Each daub showed the WG initials in the corner.

Ross Grant hastened to inspect the two double rows but his own opinion seemed to agree with Roland's. He rejoined the group within a few minutes. 'Pretty much what I expected,' he said.

'They're worthless, are they?' said Jane.

'What you see certainly is,' said Ross. He glanced around with a mixture, Roland thought, of defiance and humour. 'If anyone here is clinging to the idea that I might have turned to robbery or even to murder in order to get my hands on them, think again. But what are they painted on? You'll have to get them X-rayed. Your ancestor was quite capable of carrying off the work of much superior artists in order to cover it with his own poor efforts which, in his mind alone, were more worthy.'

'All sixty-eight?' Roland said. 'That'll not come cheap.'

'Not when you take into account insurance, security and transport.' said Ross. 'Remember, you may have big money here. Or, of course, you may not. Perhaps what you want is a major gambler, somebody like a rich Chinese who might be prepared to make a big offer for the lot on the off chance of coming across an Old Master.'

Jane was looking intrigued by the idea but Bright was not finished. He had been reading labels. He stopped at a particularly gaudy representation of a clerical gentleman with a peevish expression, evidently about to preach fire and brimstone. '*The Reverend Fergus McAulay-Trapp*,' he read out. '*Trapp!*' he repeated.

It took the company some seconds to connect the reverend gentleman with the word pencilled in the margin of the trust deed.

Roland felt impelled to guard against over-optimism. 'He – Wyvern – may only have been regretting overpainting what he regarded as his own best work and wanted to be sure that he could find it again,' he suggested.

'We can find out,' Jane said.

'They do have an X-ray facility at the cottage hospital,' Ian Fellowes said slowly. 'I remember the sounds of joy when they got it. Even common colds were being X-rayed for the first month. Run it up to the hospital,' he told Bright. 'Take it to Sister Jenkins.'

'Tell her it's for me,' said Jane. 'Remind her that I saved her cat from choking to death on a mouse that he'd tried to swallow whole.'

'I'll come with you,' said Ross. 'I might recognize something that could otherwise be missed.'

For a dozen heartbeats the group exchanged glances and telepathic messages, but there was a tacit conclusion that the association of DSgt Bright and Ross Grant would not be a fertile field for a criminal partnership and no objection was made.

While Ross Grant and Bright were on their errand, Jane was eager to speculate as to how many of Wyvern Grant's paintings might overlay Old Masters beneath. She was giving her opinion that one good painting under the *Trapp* hotchpotch would pay for all the others to be X-rayed when Ian Fellowes broke in.

'While Mr Grant's away, it's a good time to speculate as to who is the guilty party behind all these evil deeds. I'm referring to the death of your great-grandfather, the attempt to poison Mr Fox and the assault on my constable, to mention three.'

'Oh, yes.' Jane came down out of the clouds to which her dreams of wealth had raised her and which had pushed her desire to avenge GG's death into the background. The black shadow came back, stronger for the respite. It took her some seconds to return to the subject of her quest for justice. 'I told you about the cigarette ends and the dog hair, didn't I?'

'You did,' Fellowes said. 'That was good observation.'

'Well?'

'There was a report from the lab last night. They've got DNA from the smoker and hair from the dog. What they don't have yet is a person and a dog to compare them with. We've been collecting DNA samples but we hadn't got round to this particular gentleman.'

She looked at Roland.

'We can run over such characters as we know of in connection with Luke Grant, one at a time,' Roland said, 'if you think it will do any good. We can think about the very bare description furnished by the Donald girl, which only amounted to the fact that he was broad. We can take into account physical fitness and agility or a fit young friend or relative, opportunity and even, reluctantly, motive. I would suggest that Ross Grant does not fit the description at all.' Roland fought back an enormous yawn. The inhabitants of Wedell and round about all seemed such unlikely suspects. He was in for an hour or two of intolerable boredom. 'Adamson is no better a fit, he's as thin as a rake.'

'We could try for a better description,' Jane said. She took up her mobile phone. Roland quoted the now familiar number of the cottage hospital. Jane keyed it in and asked for Jessie Donald.

'Sister Donald's on her break just now.' There was a wait before Jessie Donald came on the line. While they waited, Roland asked Jane, 'Who else comes close to fitting the parameters?'

'Nobody who I've thought of so far.' A few minutes passed in discussion and rejection of less and less likely suspects. 'But if you remember that there could have been quarrels or other motives that we haven't heard of, then a dozen local – hello?' A faint quacking suggested the arrival of Sister Donald on the line.

'Ask her if Sheila's remembered any more,' Roland said.

Roland and Ian were forced to listen to one side of a discussion about a cat and then a longer discussion about what young girls got up to, especially when spending so much time with a boy. 'They only read poetry to each other,' Jane said. From the length and vehemence of Mrs Donald's comments they gathered that the nurse had doubts about where poetry could lead, but at last Jane managed to terminate the call. 'Sheila's at home, Jessie said. I hope she's right. She gave me her number.' Jane was already keying.

'Ask her if the man had a dog.'

The ringing tone was answered. 'Sheila? It's Jane Highsmith. Yes, the vet. You remember we spoke about the man in the tree? I wondered if you'd remembered any more about him.' Evidently the short reply was negative. 'Well, tell me this. Did he have a dog with him?'

There was a silence on the line until Roland feared that the connection had been broken. Then there came a spate of what he gathered to be apologies.

'It's all right,' Jane said several times, and then, 'It's easy to forget about a dog. Everybody around here has a dog. So much so that you notice anybody who walks without one. To be fair, I only asked you about the man. The important point is, was the dog well trained? Enough to sit between the boulders while his owner climbed around in the tree? What sort of dog was it? Well, describe it. Yes, you can. Surely you could at least make a guess about the breed. Labrador? Spaniel? What sort of spots? You mean like a Dalmatian?' Jane covered the receiver. 'She says no, not black spots on white but dark brown splodges and spots on a pale dog?' Her voice had risen in excitement. 'Is that right? Sheila, I think you just earned that reward.'

She disconnected. They looked at each other with what the poet called a wild surmise. 'Well done, Roland,' Jane said. 'Good guess!'

'I was remembering hearing the sound of a dog's claws on tarmac near the tree, another time,' said Roland. 'I was coming to that gentleman next.'

That single revelation could have kept them talking for days, but before they could get properly launched on the subject they were interrupted by the return of Ross Grant and DSgt Bright. The two men walked up the stairs, into an expectant silence and questioning looks too acute for words.

Answering the unspoken question Ross said, 'I don't know.'

Ian Fellowes asked, 'Wouldn't the sister play ball?'

'She was ready to play,' Ross said. 'I think she was keener than either of us to find a fresh outlet for her talents. But that X-ray setup was not designed to probe paintings. Sometimes she could get a clear picture of a tiny area at a time. More often not.' He paused, swallowed once and took a deep breath. 'I don't want to raise false hopes but I got the impression of a typical Scottish painting of the time and I got a glimpse of a small part of a signature that put me in mind of the paintings of Sir Henry Raeburn at Glasgow University. If that turns out to be correct, you're in the real money; but you'll have to send it for a more professional X-ray examination and then for restoration.'

'And how much would that cost?' Jane asked.

Ross shrugged. 'I couldn't tell you. I've never been involved in questions of authentication. But if a bookmaker went mad and offered you five hundred to one if you'd bet a thousand on the favourite for the Derby, wouldn't you take the bet?' When Jane hesitated he went on, 'Well, I'd jump at it, risking a thousand for a good chance of winning half a million. So I'll tell you what I'll do. I'll offer you one thousand pounds cash for the *Trapp* picture.'

Jane hesitated again. She raised her eyebrows at Roland. Then her jaw took on a firm line and she shook her head. 'I'll keep it,' she said.

'There you are!' Ross said, grinning. 'You've just made exactly the bet that I suggested.

TWENTY

The cottage hospital was still under pressure. Admissions were being demanded for *C.diff* patients and at the same time the complications of dealing separately with infectious and other patients were stretching resources near snapping point. Roland and Jane, however, were progressing well, aided by the healing power of comparative youth, and it was soon decided that they could be trusted to follow the hospital routine at home, aided by visits from the district nurses.

Accordingly, only three days after discovery of the paintings, they found themselves back in Jane's house. Roland felt strong enough to drive Jane's car home but Jane travelled by ambulance. They were told to rest and indeed one of the nurses relieved them by evicting from the refrigerator any food that had gone seriously off during their absence. The NHS, rising for once to the challenge, sent in a home help to undertake bed making and other tasks which were deemed to be beyond the capability of either invalid. Occupational Therapy lent them stools and other aids. They were relieved of the need to shop. They fell into a routine of helping each other. It would have been a comfortable time, but Roland was haunted by a conviction that the pieces of the puzzle did not quite fit.

They had been home for two days and were feeling much the better for it physically when in an early afternoon Ian Fellowes arrived at the door. Behind him stood a police Range Rover, bright in the sunshine. They had been starved of news and, no longer having their time and minds filled with speculation about Who? and How?, were left to wonder about Why? The detective inspector found himself seated in the sitting room with a mug of tea in his hand before he had more time than was needed to utter the barest greeting.

'This morning,' he said, 'we took Angus Holmes into

custody. Well, you knew that it had to be him – I have your assurance that he owns the only German shorthaired pointer for miles around. We arranged an identity parade and Sheila Donald picked him out straight away. We then confronted him with the laboratory tests which confirm his presence and that of his dog just as the Donald girl described and we read him Ronnie Fiddler's statement about the traces left around the bridge and the tree. He seems ready to make a statement but first he wants an interview with the two of you.'

'I suppose he wants a chance to put the gypsy's curse on us for fingering him,' Jane said.

'I don't think so. He seems to be blaming Ronnie Fiddler and the Donald girl for that, and quite rightly. But he doesn't bear much malice. I think he was already nursing a conscience about killing his old friend.'

'So he damn well should. Has he said why he did it?' Roland asked.

'Not a word so far. He insists that we meet at his house.'

'We can do that.' Jane grinned suddenly. 'I've got it! That's where the dogs are. He wants a promise that we'll see that Dram's taken care of.'

'Will you give it?' Roland asked.

'Me? I thought that you could take him on. Then you'd have a dog to work during next season.'

'You'll be needing a replacement for King Coal before too long. Of course . . . if we . . .' Roland's voice died away.

Ian Fellowes looked sharply from one to the other. He had his radio in his hand. He got up and walked outside. Roland, who knew that he could have seen the mast on the police building from a back window, knew therefore that the policeman could not possibly be having a problem with radio reception and gave him credit for unusual tact.

'I thought,' Jane said slowly, 'I thought that if you moved into Whinmount with me we could share dogs.'

'And we'd have . . .' Roland lost his nerve. 'Two houses to sell,' he said.

Jane pointed an accusing finger at him. 'You were going to say that we'd save on beds.' She got up, joined Roland on the couch and took his face in her hands. 'Poor Roland! You're not the romantic, impetuous knight that your name suggests. I'm sorry, I really am, and I hope you'll forgive me. I've been keeping you hanging on while we both knew that something good was coming. Well, I felt that I couldn't start a relationship the way it should begin while I was still preoccupied with my worry and anger over GG's death, but that's over now. I knew all along what you were feeling. I felt the same.' She kissed him slowly, fondly, warmly and then with passion. 'Whenever you feel strong enough.'

Roland was silent for some seconds while he explored his senses. 'I feel strong enough now,' he said.

Jane shook with laughter. 'This might not be a good moment, with Ian about to walk back in. Can you wait for tonight?'

'I'll try very hard.'

They had time for one more kiss before Ian returned. 'They're still at Wedell.'

Mr Holmes's Land Rover had been joined by a police Ford at the keeper's door. Inside, they found Holmes, looking strangely smaller, seated in his usual chair. His wrists were handcuffed in front of him. He nodded, without a smile or frown. DSgt Bright, notebook and pen in hand, was seated beside him. Sandy jumped up to join Roland. King Coal came to Jane more slowly but with as much affection.

'Will you keep Dram?' Holmes asked without preamble.

Roland exchanged a glance with Jane. 'I said that that would be what you wanted. Well, none of this is the dog's fault. Yes, we'll give Dram a home and work him. Maybe we can't keep him as busy as he's used to but he'll have other dogs for company and we'll do our best for him.'

Holmes blew out a sigh of relief. 'That's all I can ask. Jane, can you forgive me?' He waited anxiously.

Despite the revulsion that had grown out of his guilt, Jane had to give him credit for thinking first of Dram; and there was room in a corner of her mind for pity. The man looked haunted. Nevertheless, this was the quarry that she and Roland had hunted for days. Her hesitation stretched but the glow of a new love shone into that dark corner. 'Can you forgive yourself?' she asked.

'I don't know.'

'Nor do I.'

'But you don't hate me?'

'No, I don't hate you. I should but I'm not good at hating.'

Holmes almost smiled. But then Roland said, 'You haven't asked me.' (Holmes tried to look both surprised and innocent. It was a poor attempt.) 'You'd been in the kitchen of Jane's house that day. We'd picked the mushrooms within sight of your windows. You're the only person who had any reason to want me . . . out of the way.'

'You can't . . .' Holmes broke off within a millisecond of admitting his guilt by insisting on a lack of proof. 'I didn't,' he said. 'Whatever it is you're accusing me of. I'm not charged with anything else.'

'For the moment,' Ian Fellowes said. 'It seemed more convenient for now to charge you with the murder of Mr Luke Grant. We had the evidence and now we have your admission. With regard to the attempt to poison Mr Fox, we are looking for witnesses who saw you gathering fungi. While I was questioning you in my car, my officers were taking many, many samples from inside this house. Those samples will be tested for traces of poisonous fungi. Mr Fox saved some uncooked samples and those that were not used for purposes of analysis were sent to be examined for traces of your DNA. Samples from Miss Grant's kitchen will follow.'

Roland was well aware that he had been very ill. The facts that he had been in serious danger of death and that Holmes had been responsible while attempting to hide his own guilt had become submerged in his mind under the successful conclusion of his quest on behalf of Jane and the sudden blossoming of their new relationship. The facts were that he was alive and Holmes was in custody. Those factors had become merged together, the composite outcome being a softening of attitude.

He looked at the keeper. 'You're a bad bugger,' he said firmly.

Holmes hung his head. 'I know it.'

The abject capitulation was disarming. Even so, if Roland had not just been presented with a promise of happiness he might have pressed for the utmost retribution that the law could exact. But he could still feel Jane's lips on his. He turned his eyes to Ian Fellowes. 'The attempt on me would be a lesser charge than the actual murder of Luke Grant. These tests for DNA come expensive. In the interest of the national economy I suggest that if Mr Holmes makes a full and frank confession to the killing of Luke Grant, I might suddenly forget the circumstances surrounding the toxic fungi.'

'That,' Ian Fellowes said sternly, 'is a most improper suggestion, smacking of plea bargaining. If the evidence was there, I'm sure the procurator fiscal wouldn't hear of it.'

'But does he have to hear of it?'

The DI scratched his chin. Tying up the loose ends and presenting a well proven case was always his favourite part of a case and he was being offered the chance of a reso- lution of one case and the closure of another. 'I can't imagine the accused mentioning it,' he said weakly.

Bright knew too well who would be left to gather up the evidence. Poisoning is comparatively easy to prove but pinning the guilt on an individual may be much more diffi- cult. His mouth was sealed.

Roland was looking forward to gathering background for a future novel. He wanted to sample the atmosphere of a murder trial, follow the intricacies of argument, observe procedures and take note of terminology. He thought that any sentence imposed additional to the one for GG's murder would probably be concurrent rather than consecutive. The confession would shorten proceedings considerably but there would still be the speeches. 'I want to be a spectator, not a witness,' he explained. Jane mimed zipping her lips.

The keeper straightened up. 'You both like a choice cut of pork, I think.'

Ian Fellowes had indulged in enough mercy for one day. 'You can't give your pigs away,' the DI said quickly. 'I'll have to bring them to the attention of the meat inspector.'

Roland could not decide whether the keeper's expression was a smile or a sneer. 'I know that fine,' Holmes said. 'But I've a freezer full of good pork and they can help themselves. Take the dog food and anything else that's perishable. And speak to the agent who lets your house for you and see can he find me a good tenant. I'd like to feel that this house will be waiting for me when I come out. But keep back the garage to store anything I'd want to keep. You may as well have the use of my Land Rover.' He looked at Jane. 'You have a shotgun certificate, I think? Will you take charge of my gun for me? I can sign it over to you meantime. It's another old friend I'd not want to part with.'

Jane could feel the inspector's eyes boring into her but she lifted her chin. 'You've got a bloody nerve. We'll look after Dram,' she said, 'but that's for his sake, not yours. And I'll look after your gun and have it put on to my certificate. But the agent would expect the house to be cleaned and cleared of your personal odds and ends. We don't owe you anything. Quite the reverse. If we're to consider for one moment doing all you're asking, the least you can do is to tell us why you killed my very dear great-grandfather. I think we know what you did and how you did it. But why, for God's sake? You didn't know anything about the pictures, did you?'

Holmes's puzzlement looked genuine. 'Pictures? I don't know about any pictures.' He sighed. There was no trace of his former arrogance. He looked forlorn and despite her anger, despite the desire for retribution that had driven her to hunt him out, Jane's heart was touched as if by a wounded animal.

'Tell us, then,' she said gently. 'You owe me that much.'

'I owe you that much and more and I've already admitted what I did.' Holmes heaved a sigh that came right up from his bowels. 'All right, then. It was over a woman, of course. Your great-granddad was old, too old to get it up any more, I think, but he still had looks and manners and the voice and all the things that send shivers up a woman's back, so I'm told. Miss James, now. There's a damn fine woman.'

'Mrs Cadwallader's companion?' Roland exclaimed.

'You saw how she joined in and helped when we were

carrying Dram back here. That was typical of her. When I had the flu last winter she nursed me and fed me and she did the round of my traps. You may not have seen her smile but it's kind and generous and it can warm a room or calm an angry beast.' He smacked the arm of his chair, although the impediment of the handcuff robbed the gesture of much of its force. 'She'd have made a grand wife for a keeper instead of companion for that fat sow. But when I asked her, she said . . .'

Jane could not stop herself from asking the question. 'What did she say?'

'She said that she couldn't see past your great-granddad. But I think now that that may just have been a story, because after he . . . died . . . I asked her again and this time she said there was still somebody else. Mrs Cadwallader has a nephew who visits her from time to time and I think there's some carrying-on there, which they wouldn't admit in case the old biddy cut him out of her will. And now I'm hearing that he's to marry a girl from Kelso.' He met Jane's eye. 'So it was all for nothing. And you were so good to Dram, not knowing what I'd done. If you'd known, would you still . . . ?'

'I would never leave an animal to suffer,' Jane said. She got up and left the house quickly to hide her tears.

The keeper was not so concerned to hide his feelings. Because of the handcuffs he had some difficulty extracting a large coloured handkerchief from his pocket to bury his face in. Dram rolled cautiously to his feet, quitted his basket and came to lay his head on the keeper's knee. The attempt at consolation was too much. The keeper lowered his brow onto the dog's with his handkerchief between and gave a sob. 'What a waste!' he said. 'What a bloody waste!'

Dram, uncomprehending but sympathetic, tried to lick his face and got a mouthful of handkerchief for his trouble.

While Holmes dictated a rambling confession to DSgt Bright, Roland retired to the sunshine outside, beckoning Jane and Fellowes to accompany him. Further along the wall of Wedell but away from windows there was a seat of solid teak overlooking the garden and they settled there. The Adamsons' children were romping at the far end of the garden, beyond earshot.

'We have two criminals,' Roland said. 'That's what's been throwing me – I've been trying to fit one person to all the misdeeds. But it wasn't like that.' In his concentration his usually precise English was slipping. 'Holmes killed Mr Grant and tried to poison me.'

Ian Fellowes said, 'Yes.'

'Somebody else was after the paintings.'

'Yes.' The DI was nursing a secret smile. 'We made another arrest yesterday morning.'

Roland managed to refrain from grinding his teeth or showing other signs of frustration. 'Who?' he said. 'Who?' He tried not to sound like an owl that he had heard and which Jane had identified for him.

'This is in absolute confidence. My constable says that his attacker was not a large man. He insists that he was small and skinny with it. *Nairra-boukit* was the expression he used, but he comes from somewhere in the wilds up near Huntley. The point is that we could believe him. The human tendency is to remember an attacker as larger than life. That pointed the finger at either—'

'Adamson or Ross Grant,' Roland said. 'Even I had got that far. But which?'

The DI was not going to be hurried. 'As it happened, the lab had got some good DNA off the rolling-pin and it matched one of the samples we'd been taking in connection with the murder of Luke Grant. I had just received that report when Ross Grant walked in and asked to see me.'

'To confess?'

The DI smiled with satisfaction. 'Certainly not. He said that he had only just heard about the constable being attacked and he felt that there was something that he should tell us. During his conversations with Adamson about history and particularly the history of art, Adamson had been fishing for information about Wyvern Grant. Adamson had been tracking the artist in the diaries of his contemporaries and had found references to an unholy row that occurred because

Grant had pinched a finished work by one of the big names at the time and put one of his own daubs over the top of it. Unfortunately, from your point of view, the scandal had been hushed up and there was no mention of the identity of the big name.'

'Nor of the portrait that he laid over it?' Jane asked.

'Nor that either. I fetched Adamson in for questioning. He tried to invent credible explanations for the presence of his DNA on the rolling-pin but failed. In the end he admitted that he was pushed for money to feed all those children and he had coveted the painting for the money it would fetch. He had no clue as to which canvas it was on but the word *Trap* had been mentioned.'

'And,' said Roland, 'no doubt he will say that he expected the house to be empty but he picked up the rolling pin to use as a threat if anybody challenged him, but when he found himself confronted by a figure larger than himself, he couldn't see any uniform in the dim light and he lost his head and lashed out. He apologized to your constable and would like to make it up to him.'

'You must be bloody psychic,' said Inspector Fellowes.

TWENTY-ONE

Holmes had already admitted setting the trap that killed Luke Grant but his counsel made the most of the facts. Like thousands before him, the keeper was a man betrayed by a friend and fooled by a woman, more sinned against than sinning. He was a caring person who cared for the wildlife around him and reared his birds as though they were his children. He had been celibate, living a monastic life, so that when Cupid's dart struck he was an easy victim and deeply regretted his rash action. The judge had heard it all before but the jury had not. His regrets were accepted as sincere and the jury made a recommendation for mercy. This must have carried some weight with the judge because the sentence was the minimum that the law allows. Miss James visits him regularly, taking Dram with her by special arrangement with the warden of the open prison. Dram has settled for the moment at Whinmount and his occasional visits to his master seem to reassure him.

Jane Highsmith and Roland Fox are happy together in Whinmount. They have not yet married. They are putting off that expense until there are the first signs of the family for which they are trying so pleasurably and so hard. Jane has her veterinary practice and Roland's second book was purchased for television, so money would not be short but for the paintings.

A garish portrait of Patrick Ferguson was found to overlay a painting of Edinburgh Castle by Angus Dutton, a painter well placed in the second rank of Scottish artists. It realized just enough money to pay for its own uncovering and for that of the supposed Raeburn painting. The experts are still arguing, expensively, as to whether the latter is genuine Raeburn or 'school of'.